THE LADIES' ROOM

THE LADIES' ROOM

KAYT C. PECK

SAPPHIRE BOOKS

SALINAS, CALIFORNIA

The Ladies' Room
Copyright © 2015 by Kayt C. Peck. All rights reserved.

ISBN - 978-1-943353-09-5

Editor - CK King
Book Design - LJ Reynolds
Cover Design - Michelle Brodeur

Sapphire Books
Salinas, CA 93912
www.sapphirebooks.com

Printed in the United States of America
First Edition – September 2015

This and other Sapphire Books titles can be found at
www.sapphirebooks.com

Dedication

In memory of a place called Sassy's and in honor of the courageous colleagues who helped form OUTstanding Amarillo. I've never been prouder to be a part of anything.

Acknowledgments

Much thanks to "The Boss" at Sapphire Books. Without her this story and many others might never see the light of day.

Chapter One

Reflected light danced across the floor, ignoring completely the rhythm of the Garth Brooks number begging for a snappy two-step. The joy of the light shone from the mirrored ball suspended from the ceiling, not at all dimmed by the fact that the dance floor was empty. Well, not completely empty. There was a layer of cornmeal, freshly scattered by Bart, the Tuesday night dance instructor.

"He's got gumption. I'll give him that," Tandy Johnson said, as she lifted April Sims's elbow from the bar so she could polish the worn wood beneath.

April looked up from her beer to study the handsome young man who now shuffled alone on the dance floor, testing the slickness provided by the cornmeal. He moved with liquid grace despite the lack of a partner. April admired the pure beauty of motion, as Bart switched from a simple two-step to a pattern she hadn't a prayer of recognizing…or repeating.

"I take it the dance lessons aren't a big hit," April said, her voice raised over the music.

Tandy ran stubby fingers through short, red hair salted with gray. "I warned him Tuesday night was a killer. He must have taken it as a challenge."

April watched the graceful young man test the dance floor. His movements communicated impatient confidence.

"Doesn't seem too discouraged to me," April

said.

"Damned if you're not right. We had five people show up first night, and three the second."

"This the third?"

"Yeah. If nobody shows at all, guess I'll have to tell him to give it up. Hate to. Truth is, he gives darned good dance lessons."

April lifted her longneck, draining the last of the beer from the bottom. Tandy took the bottle, but didn't offer another. In the six years they'd known each other, Tandy had rarely seen April drink more than one beer at a sitting and never more than two. At first, the older woman respected the habit as a religious conviction. Then, one night playing gin rummy at Tandy and Sharon's house, April dared to down three beers. They didn't even finish the hand before April laid her head on the table and interrupted the conversation with her snores. When they had the irresistible urge to tease, as friends tend to do, Tandy and Sharon needed only to softly imitate a snore to send them both into fits of giggles, and turn April's face red. Tandy watched the effects of beer on April, and April watched the effects of time on Tandy. April figured it was an even swap.

The music ended, and Bart left the floor to walk up a short flight of stairs to the DJ's booth. The two women listened to the click of plastic, as he rummaged through CD cases, selecting music for the dance lessons already late in starting…for the dance lessons currently lacking a vital element, students.

April rammed her hands into the pockets of her brown leather jacket and fiddled absently with the pen inside. She always had a pen and a pad stashed somewhere. As a reporter, pens and paper were as much a part of her life as computers and cameras, crooks and politicians.

The familiar feel of a cheap ballpoint gave nervous fingers something to do. She played with the idea of asking Bart to help her polish a waltz, but, as much as she wanted to help the energetic young man, she just didn't feel like dancing. Truth was, she resented the blare of the music, the bright lights. She'd not come to the Pink Triangle for music and laughs. She came because she needed the simple company of a good friend, an old friend, a friend who could feel her mood and ease the soreness even if April couldn't define its source. Being alone was hard some nights.

"For as long as I've know you, you've complained about Tuesday nights," April said. "If business is so bad, why don't you just close?"

Tandy polished a section of the bar that was already polished. "If a person goes into business, they should be in business for real, not just when it's convenient."

"Nobody would care, Tandy. Hell, we're just tickled pink to have a women's bar in Amber."

Tandy's eye's narrowed and she shook the limp end of a damp bar towel at April. "You tell me, April Sims. When is it you come see me?"

April chewed at her lip as she thought. "I play cards with you and Sharon on Sunday afternoons."

"I ain't talking about that, and you know it."

"No, I don't. Explain."

Tandy leaned close, as close as she could force her bulk over the edge of the bar. "When you want to talk, when you need ears to listen, when do you come see me?"

April looked across the dance floor, her mood

freshly blackened. "On Tuesday nights."

"You're not alone." Tandy turned her back to stack glasses in a rack. "When you own a bar, especially a 'family' bar, you offer more than liquor and music. For twenty years I've served the drinks, washed the glasses, and heard the dreams and fears of the queers of Amber, Texas." Tandy pointed with a stocky, square jaw toward the empty room with shabby tables and uneven chairs. "The Pink Triangle is more than a bar." She filled one rack, placed another empty one on top, and began filling it in turn. Her face was fierce as she turned to her friend. "Who you work with every day?"

"You know who I work with. You've met half of them."

"List a few."

"Let's see, you probably know Slider the best. He's the only one brave enough to go to a gay bar. Then there's my editor Sam Trimble. You know Kate Stevens…now, who else?"

"Forget who else. Just tell me one thing. What do they all have in common?"

"They're journalists."

"What else?"

"Damn it, Tandy. I'm tired of twenty questions. What're you saying?"

The intensity of Tandy's green eyes grew to a level that made many folks stutter and stumble.

"They're straight, or at least pretending to be, every doggone one of them. If you…if this town didn't have the Pink Triangle and the Tickled Texan, Amber wouldn't have a gay community. You'd be just another lonely dyke wondering who else was out there. Wondering if you were completely alone."

April blinked back tears, ashamed of how little

she'd appreciated Tandy's simple watering hole.

"Is that the way it was?"

"Why do you think I opened the bar?"

A bubble of pride in her crusty friend pushed through April's dark mood. In two quick moves, April was on top of the bar and planting a long, noisy kiss on the top of Tandy's head.

"God bless you, Tandy Johnson, you hard-assed, old, country girl, you."

"Darn you! I just cleaned that bar." Tandy blushed with pleasure.

April ignored her friend and firmly planted her butt on the bar. She looked around the room with a new perspective.

"Is it right?" April asked.

"What?"

"Not that I don't appreciate the Pink Triangle, but this is a place of beer and smoke, and I've seen more lust than love shuffling on that dance floor."

"What you saying, girl?"

"Is this what we are? Can any community be healthy if the only place it can meet is a bar?"

April was shocked to see a long, slow smile grow across Tandy's face.

"What you grinning about?" April asked.

"I've waited fifteen years for somebody to ask that question." There was a greedy look in Tandy's eyes.

April slid off the bar, moving easily back to her seat on the barstool. A sense of foreboding showed on her face.

"What you up to, Tandy Johnson?"

Tandy threw her soiled bar rag onto the counter and lifted the gate that was her only exit from her usual duty station. She stripped off her apron and threw it onto the bar.

"Hey, Bart!"

"Yo," the dance teacher answered, his head popping up over the edge of the DJ's box.

"Watch the bar, will you?"

"I can't mix drinks."

"You can draw beer, can't you? If they want anything else, tell 'em I'll be back in a few minutes."

Bart nodded agreement and returned to shuffling through compact disc cases. April stayed on her seat, as Tandy strode across the floor, headed for the side entrance. Tandy halted and turned toward her friend.

"You coming or aren't you?" Tandy asked gruffly.

April's foreboding had grown into mild anxiety.

"Coming where?" she asked.

"Just get your ass off that barstool and get over here," Tandy demanded.

Six years of friendship made it a difficult demand to ignore. Besides, curiosity was even deadlier for a journalist than for the proverbial cat. She went, shuffling hesitantly after Tandy's confident stride. April's mystification grew as Tandy led her out the side entrance, up a flight of exterior stairs, and then stopped beside a neglected, second-floor door. Tandy rummaged through an oversized set of keys she'd brought from behind the bar.

"Why the hell we going to the storeroom?" April asked.

"It's not a storeroom," Tandy answered, not looking up from the fistful of keys.

April studied the door. Its paint was chipped, and the knob was tarnished. It looked like a storeroom door. In all the years she'd patronized the Pink

Triangle, this was April's first trip up the exterior stairs. Sometime during the first year or two, she'd ceased to even see those stairs.

"That's it." Tandy selected a key and clicked it into the lock. The door opened, and Tandy flicked the light switch and led April into a long-neglected, dust-filled room. Two couches and several chairs, all covered with dustcloths, were scattered around the room. Two small tables, with four chairs each, rested against the wall. The only cover protecting them from new dust was the thick layer of earlier dust. It was substantial.

"What's this?" April asked.

"An old dream," Tandy answered.

"I've never heard you talk about this place."

"It hurt too much. Bothered me for a long time that the idea failed. Ask Sharon."

"So, what was the idea that failed?" April encouraged.

"I wanted a place where women could...well... just be together. No music, no drinks, and, hopefully, not so many of the games you see down in the bar. About ten years ago, I opened up this room, furnished it from the Salvation Army, and just left it open, a retreat for whoever wanted to get away from the bar."

"I take it didn't work out."

The creases deepened in Tandy's face. "Royal disaster. It was rarely used, except as a make out haven, and it became something of a joke. One night, I came up here to check on it and found a straight pair of teenagers fucking their brains out. That's when I closed it down."

April moved around the room, studying it with her eyes and mind. She played with Tandy's vision of a place to build a community, a place where women, lovers of women, could share, nurture, and heal. She liked it. She liked the feel and the smell of it, despite the dust.

"So, why'd you bring me up her, old friend?" April asked in a hushed whisper.

"When I shut this place down, it was with the dream of reopening it when the time was right."

"And now…you think the time is right?"

Tandy's eyes narrowed. "Maybe, maybe not. I think I've finally found what it needed to survive."

"And what's that?"

"Somebody…somebody with the dream, vision, and drive to make it work. Without someone's heart and soul poured into this…" Tandy gestured at the dust and second hand furniture, "…it's just another empty room."

The sense of foreboding returned to April. "And you think I'm that person?"

A sly smile teased at the corners of Tandy's mouth. "I been watching you rattle around since Amanda left."

April blushed at the mention of her former lover. It still stung nearly two years after Amanda left her for a new life and a new love.

"You need something," Tandy continued. "And it's not just another woman. You need a purpose, a drive, something other than your work to make you get up in the morning."

April shuffled her feet, uncomfortable with the stinging truth of Tandy's observation.

"And you got what it takes," Tandy added. "You can deal with people, and you know how to use words better than anyone I know."

As Tandy spoke, the dust and neglect of the room ceased to be the predominant feature to April. Tandy's dream was contagious.

"I'll think about it," April said.

"That's all I can ask."

April drew a line in the dust atop one of the tables. "Did the place have a name?" she asked.

"I called it the Upper Room. I think that was part of the problem."

April laughed. "Lord yes. What were you thinking? Do something that even hints at religion, and you lose most gays."

"Too many of us burned by the Bible thumpers, I guess."

There was a comfortable silence as the two friends let the idea of their venture grow. A thought sent a slow, half-devious smile across April's face.

"What's getting at you?" Tandy asked.

"I got a name."

"What?"

"It's for women only, right?"

"Suppose so."

A twinkle in her eyes joined April's smile. "Let's call it the Ladies' Room."

"Well, since the signs in the Pink Triangle say 'The John' and 'The Joan,' there shouldn't be any confusion," Tandy answered.

April chuckled. "I guess it says a lot about our community, when we both think our folks would rather a meeting place be named after a toilet than a holy place."

Tandy yanked up a dust cover and shook the filthy cloth. The cloud that followed made them both cough.

"If time and hearts are right, even a toilet can be holy," the older woman said.

April heard a ring of truth somewhere in her heart.

Chapter Two

Y ou don't need a cleanup crew. You need a demolition team," Mo Thompson said as she stood, transfixed, just two feet inside the door. Without ceremony, she dropped the plastic bucket she carried. The bottle of glass cleaner tipped out among a handful of cleaning rags.

The rest of April's softball buddies gathered around Mo, a woman who was their unofficial leader even when they weren't on the field. They stared at the neglect and devastation around them, their faces reflecting the amazement Mo expressed so clearly. They stood crowded together in a huddle of women, brooms, buckets, and mops.

"Girlfriend, my granddaddy wouldn't turn a mule into a place this bad," Johnnie Johnson said, as she studied a crusted stain of questionable origin on a ragged square of carpet.

Sally "Billboard" Jones used a putty knife to brush a substantial pile of mouse turds from a counter. "That beer I said you had to buy me just turned into a six-pack."

April faced her teammates and friends. "Come on, guys. Just have a little vision."

Mo kicked a sheet-covered couch and watched the clouds of dust her action raised.

"Might look better if we was downright blind," Mo said in disgust.

A freckled-faced boy of ten walked to the counter of what had once been a kitchen and stared into a stained and chipped sink. He turned on the tap and waited as the pipes rattled and banged until a fitful flow of brown water finally erupted from the spigot.

"If you want me to touch this, somebody's gonna hafta raise my allowance," Mo's nephew demanded.

April strode to his side and laid her arm across his shoulder.

"How about a two-Superman-comic bonus, Bubba?"

"Maybe," he said as the stream progressed, looking more like water. His sister wasn't as easily convinced.

"I'm not thirsty anymore," little Morrie said as she stood on tiptoe, looking cautiously into the sink. Without a word, April reached into the cooler she'd hauled up the stairs and handed the child a Pepsi. Morrie's face brightened, and April felt she had her first convert.

"Tell me again why we're doing this," said Mo's sister. Allison, the only heterosexual in the team's core group of players, was frequently the voice of sanity. Nobody knew if it was because she was straight, or because of her years of practice keeping Mo on track and out of trouble. Still others thought motherhood served as her secret to wisdom.

"Listen, gang. Don't look at this as a dirty dump..."

"Lordy, Lordy, now she's leading us to fantasy," Johnnie mumbled.

"...but see what it will be," April continued, ignoring her friend. "Imagine what this place can do." Excitement grew in her voice as she tried to instill the flash of a dream she shared with Tandy. It didn't seem as clear in the light of day and surrounded by doubting friends, but the dream still lived.

Mo walked to April and stood so close April could smell the pizza odor that still hung to Mo's clothes from lunch.

"April, hon, I'm just a simple woman. I'm a damn good track coach, and I can even teach a little math, but if Sis over there hadn't ragged my ass to finish college, I wouldn't even be qualified to do that." She punched April lightly on the arm. "I don't see what the hell you're talking about." A smile softened her words. "I don't believe in your dream. Hell, I don't even understand it, but I'll tell you what I do believe in."

"What?" April asked, fighting to hide her disappointment.

"I believe in you." Mo walked briskly to the sink, her bucket of rags and cleaning solution in tow. "Come on, folks. Let's get to work."

They worked like it was the playoff finals of the year. April hadn't seen that kind of concentration on Billboard Jones's face since the team's power hitter pushed in the two winning runs for the league championship. She'd led the team to victory by, once again, hitting her favorite target with her homerun swing. Billboard gained her nickname because she so loved to hear the thump of the ball on the fading billboard for Adams Brothers Funeral Home where it stood behind left field.

The same humor, the same camaraderie, that carried the Diamonds through game after game, season after season, transformed a nearly impossible cleaning mission into a productive and pleasant

Saturday afternoon. Grime gradually disappeared from walls, floors, and countertops, but an inordinate amount of the filth reappeared on the worker's faces.

Midafternoon Tandy appeared, along with her lover, Sharon. The two women struggled up the stairs, welcomed bearers of a Number 10 wash tub filled with beer, soft drinks, and ice. The newcomers admired the progress through tired eyes. Tandy's face was still softened by sleep, having just awakened from a day's rest, a fact of life for the owner of a nightclub. Sharon's exhaustion resulted from a fourteen-hour shift at the hospital.

"You folks sure made a difference in here," Tandy said.

Sharon slowly turned, taking in every corner of the room. "Tandy, honey, this looks better than it did ten years ago." She turned to face her lover. "Wish I could say the same for you," she said with a teasing smile.

Surprised laughter tittered through the room. Everybody looked wide-eyed at the tall, quiet blonde. Sharon rarely spoke, and this circle of friends was amazed at her effort to tease her gregarious lover. April, who knew the couple best, had glimpsed Sharon's playful side. She knew it as a sign of deep happiness. April also suspected exhaustion had cracked Sharon's studied reserve. Besides, Sharon may share more of Tandy's dream for the Ladies' Room than April realized.

Tandy laughed as she drew a cigarette from the crumpled packet in her shirt pocket.

"A few wrinkles just adds to my character."

Sharon put an arm around her lover's shoulders and planted a soft kiss in Tandy's red-gray hair. "I agree," the exhausted nurse-practioner said. She leaned heavily against her lover, and Tandy wrapped her arms protectively around the taller woman's waist.

"Sorry to desert you ladies, but we'd best go home. My honey hasn't slept in nearly nineteen hours," Tandy said.

"Put her to bed," Mo instructed.

"You got a good woman to take care of…you don't need to be messing with this lot," Johnnie added.

"Thanks for the drinks," April called.

Billboard waved goodbye with the tip of the longneck Bud Dry she'd just downed and burped a merry farewell. Allison and her two children called goodbye from their seats around a table, where she explained to her kids why the women looked like they had plastic hair in every photo of the 1965 *Time* magazine they'd found inside a cabinet. Seven-year-old Morrie stared wide-eyed at the photos, certain she'd discovered a tidbit of ancient history.

April plopped, filthy and tired, to a seat on the couch, just inches from where Johnnie rested. Johnnie had declared that her career as a domestic was over.

"If you folks want to scrub until there's no tile on the floor or skin on your fingers, you go right ahead." I'll just sit here and enjoy watching white folks work, and I'll just sip on this here Dr Pepper."

As usual, Johnnie was a woman of her word. She enjoyed her soft drink without a hint of guilt, as the other women worked around her. She stretched comfortably on the couch and read the Saturday paper she'd brought along with her share of cleaning supplies.

"If you'd plopped your butt on this couch like that two hours ago, we'd both be drowning in dust,"

Johnnie said, as she leaned close to April.

"Thank God for vacuum cleaners," April answered.

With the ease of long acquaintance, Johnnie placed her hand over April's. The gesture was friendly rather than sexual. In the years they'd known each other, April and Johnnie had tap danced around a relationship, had even slept together a time or two, but they both knew in their heart of hearts that they were meant to be friends.

"So, you think we done good?" Johnnie asked.

"Done good? I think we've got a spot on the USA Olympic Cleaning Team," April answered.

"I'll volunteer as coach," Mo said from where she rested on another couch. "That way I can sit on the bench and tell you all what to do."

"And I'll be the power scrubber," Billboard said, as she sipped at her second beer.

Johnnie looked at her hand intertwined with April's and let out a high-pitched squeal that made them all sit upright.

"Look at that!" she said.

April did as instructed and stared at their hands. *"What? What?"* She drew her hand to her face and looked closely, first at the palms and then the upper sides of each hand. "You see a tick or something?"

"No, look at them together," Johnnie said, placing her hand beside April's.

April focused and began to chuckle deeply. Every person in the room gathered around the two women, staring at their hands.

Patiently, April and Johnnie held their hands extended, letting everyone see the contrast. The same grime that left patches of dark on April's hand appeared on the skin of her black friend as a light film. It was as though they stared at a positive and a negative, side by side.

"There's got to be some deep, symbolic meaning to this, but I'm too tired to think what it might be," April said.

"The only meaning I see is that you both need to wash your hands," Allison the Practical said.

Morrie wiggled to a seat between April and Johnnie and held a hand from each woman in her lap, studying the difference. April felt a sense of rightness as she saw a child's trusting touch of friends from two races. Morrie dropped April's hand, and picked up Johnnie's to study it more closely.

"Your fingernails look white," the child said.

"That's 'cause there's darker skin all around," Johnnie answered.

Morrie looked again, her small forehead creasing in deep thought. "What's it like to be black?" she asked.

"Morrie!" Allison called, horrified at her daughter's boldness.

Johnnie laughed. "It's just fine. Sounds like an honest question to me." The woman used her free hand, the one not currently scrutinized by a small child, to brush a curl of hair from Morrie's eyes. "Child, I don't know that I can answer that question. Being black is with you from the time you're born until the time you die. I don't think about it much. Don't guess you think much about what it's like to be white."

The child dropped Johnnie's hand and chewed at her lower lip as she thought. "No. I never have. I'm just Morrie, I guess."

"And I'm just Johnnie."

"Jeez, you ask some of the dumbest questions,"

Bubba said to his little sister."

"Do not," she challenged.

"Do too."

"Not."

"Do."

"Enough!" Mo yelled. Halting the childish argument before it shredded all their tired nerves.

Johnnie raised the newspaper and waved it at her friends. "I wish everybody could accept different folks as easy as Morrie."

"What's up?" Mo asked.

"Wait until you see the editorial page. There's a doozy of a letter to the editor, talking about all us dykes and faggots," Johnnie answered.

"Spare us the views of the ignorant and the opinionated," Allison added.

April groaned. "Great! That means Slider will razz me big time on Monday morning. He loves showing me all the homophobes' letters. Likes to use them to prove how lucky I am to have such an open-minded friend and co-worker."

"Read it," Mo said. "I want to know what we're up against."

Johnnie folded back the paper until the letter rested before her. She read in a clear voice, only slightly tinged with the country accent of her central Texas farm folks.

"As a man of God, I remind the people of Amber that we must guard against the works of the devil. I am horrified to learn that our safe, God-fearing community is home to a growing number of the worst of Satan's helpers: homosexuals. I hate the dirty feel it gives me to even write the word.

"The Bible tells us clearly in Romans 1:24-27 that homosexuals are an abomination. As Christians we must not allow them to live among us. They do the work of the Devil and will bring nothing but grief to our community.

"I call on you all to root out this evil. They must be converted to the true life or told to take their ungodly ways elsewhere."

In God's truth,
Reverend Ralph Thomas

As Johnnie's words came to a halt, there was a silence that grew into an uncomfortable weight.

"Don't that chill your insides?" Mo finally said, breaking the silence.

"Does it say what church this guy is from?" April asked.

Johnnie glanced at the paper. "No. Some hard-liner, born-again bunch, I reckon."

Morrie went to her aunt and curled into Mo's lap, her arms tight around the woman's neck.

"Is he talking about lesbians?" the little girl asked. With a loving aunt so far out of the closet she had a hard time finding a place to hang her clothes, Morrie learned at a young age the rudiments of truth about homosexuality.

"Yeah, Morrie. He's talking about lesbians and gay men."

"Why's he hate you, Aunt Mo?"

"Don't know, sweetie. Wish I did."

Johnnie sat forward and looked at the child. "Your aunt's kind of lucky, Morrie."

"Why?" the little girl asked.

"You asked me what it was like to be black. I

guess one of the biggest things to live with is knowing that you're different from the white world everybody thinks is normal."

"Yeah?" Morrie didn't understand.

"It's not bad being different. In some ways it's better. Life being a little tougher makes us work harder and makes us prouder when we manage to get something done. It also makes us pull together. If I walk into a room full of people and there's one other black person, we're family right from the start, no matter what our other differences."

"So?" the child asked.

"Most white folks don't know about that, but gay people do." Johnnie leaned back and took April's hand once again. "Sometimes, that helps bridge the gap between white and black."

April squeezed the hand that held her own. "I hope so."

Billboard walked to the Number 10 and retrieved another longneck from the ice. "I bet that old toad doesn't drink beer either."

"He probably just looks at it as one more cross to bear," Mo answered.

"How many have you had, anyway?" Allison asked.

Billboard grinned and raised the bottle to her lips. "Don't worry. I ain't driving." She looked around the room. "I got friends to get me home."

April felt a haze of warmth around her heart. She hoped that the afternoon was a hint of the magic still to grow in the Ladies' Room.

Chapter Three

Telephone poles flew past like rows of sentries, forever guarding their little patch of soil. April fought the urge to watch the hypnotic rise and fall of telephone lines, as they climbed to the top of each pole only to fall into the valley between. It was an old routine, one she'd used to lull herself to sleep as a child on long trips in the backseat of her parents' car.

Lulling herself to sleep was not the wisest plan of action. Today, she was driving.

"I just don't get it," Theodore "Slider" Hopkins said, as he extracted the chewing gum he'd been working since they left the office. With a flourish he tossed the wadded mass out the open window.

"Some bird's probably going to choke to death on that," April said.

"Naw, it's biodegradable," Slider answered.

"The heck it is."

"It always rots off the bottom of my shoe," Slider argued.

"Does not. If you didn't scrape a bit off every step, it would be there forever," April countered. She loved these little debates with Slider.

"Okay, okay! I'll wrap it in paper and put it in the trash next time." Slider ran artistic fingers through long, thinning hair. "You queers are always uptight about some issue or another."

"Hey! This is the only environment we've got. It won't take care of us if we don't take care of it."

Slider sighed. "I'm taking my beer cans to the recycling center. What more do you want?"

April reached across to chuck her co-worker on the shoulder. "I knew you'd learn if I bugged you long enough."

The photographer shook his head and lapsed into silence, his face reflecting the morose expression habitual to him. That very look prevented many from bothering to get to know him. April considered herself lucky. Her work forced her to spend time in the company of this lanky, critical man who remained studiously oblivious to what people thought, or so she'd believed. That was before they became a team. That was before she learned to recognize the glow of pride hidden behind Slider's frown as someone admired yet another of his prize-winning, news photos. That was before she'd gained his trust and experienced her own ability to instill a glow of hurt in Slider's hound-dog brown eyes. Being Slider's friend involved a difficult dance with the exchange of verbal abuse that was Slider's favorite conversational form and the hazard of hurting this secretly sensitive man. Few people attempted the dance. Even fewer mastered it.

Slider's talent made his position with the newspaper secure, but his social position hovered near the netherworld. With the possible exception of the publisher, no single individual was better known by all 120 employees of the *Amber Daily News*. Slider's notoriety was a dubious distinction. Many laughed at his too-short jeans and perpetually white socks, and some of the news staff failed to include him in party invitations. His talent for unintentional insult made the atmosphere tense when he attended a social gathering.

April saw a different side. In the years they had worked together, they'd developed a rhythm that made them one of the best writer and photographer teams in the state. She saw the world differently now, just from the mental exercise of anticipating what Slider would discover through a camera's viewfinder. Slider's creative process fascinated her.

Besides, April knew she could depend on Slider. He'd held her head when she'd puked by the roadside, as they covered a five-car pileup including the headless body of a woman whose car had gone under a semitrailer. They'd worked together to pull an exhausted fireman to safety when he'd collapsed trying to exit a burning building. April and Slider shared a history, an important building block for trust.

People could say what they wanted. Slider was April's friend, and she was proud of it.

"I still don't get it," Slider said, breaking the silence.

April shook her head, trying to recall to what it was Slider referred. "What the hell you talking about?" she asked.

"This lesbian room you're fixing up."

"The Ladies' Room."

"Yeah." Slider shook his head. "Jeez, what a name. So, tell me why you're doing it."

April shrugged. Despite her talent with words, she still had difficulty describing the dream, especially to a pugnacious, heterosexual man.

"We just want a place to meet that isn't all loud music and alcohol."

"What're you going to do there?"

"Talk mostly."

"Sounds like some sort of support group," Slider said.

April paused in thought. "Yeah, I guess that's what it is."

"You don't think you're sick or screwed up, do you?"

"No, of course not."

"Then why do you need a support group?" he asked.

April looked at him, puzzled. "Don't you ever feel the need to…" she waved her hand, searching for the right word, "…grow."

"What the hell does that mean?"

April took her gaze from the road and looked at her friend. "Never mind," she responded.

"Hey, I don't have to understand. If it's something you need to do, more power to you, but as your friend, I advise your gang to keep your heads low," Slider said.

"Why?"

"You read the letters to the editor on Sunday?"

"You mean that one from some nutzoid preacher?"

"That's the one. Bruce Wilson from sports knows the guy. He says he's a bad one who can get his congregation to do anything he says."

"Yeah, well, we don't try to stuff what we are down people's throats, but I'm not going to let some nut force me into hiding."

April had grown uncomfortable with the conversation. She was relieved when they arrived at Angusville. She drove directly to the city hall, as

Slider checked his camera and the supply of lenses in his photojournalist's vest. A small crowd of Hispanics waited outside—enjoying the last of the day's sunshine—to face a meeting that many of them would not understand. There would be no Spanish translation. April knew why they were there. The same debate motivated April and Slider to make the sixty-mile drive to the agricultural community on the edge of the *Amber Daily* distribution area. The handful of leather-faced farm workers were there to fight for their tenuous hold on property worth little, but still more than they could afford.

"*Buenas dias*," April said, as she stepped from the car.

Members of the group mumbled a greeting, unsure of this *gringa* who welcomed them in Spanish. April took a deep breath, gathering her courage as she always did before using her textbook Spanish. She gave her name as she pulled a press card from her wallet and offered it as identification. One man took the card from her hand and studied it. April did not blame him for his caution.

"*Por favor. Podemos tomar unas fotos de ustedes?*" April waved toward Slider as she asked permission to take photographs. There was no legal reason for April to ask. The group waited in a public place for a public meeting, but she felt that courtesy was especially important. This tiny group of protesters had dared to enter a foreign place. Their courage merited respect and patience from the visiting journalists.

As a group, every person looked to the man who still held April's press card. After a moment's hesitation, the man searched April's eyes for some hint of her character. He finally nodded agreement as he returned the card to April's hand. April took the press card and handed the man a business card in return.

It was well the man agreed. Slider was already kneeling before an *abuela* where the old woman sat atop a concrete planter, patiently waiting to enter the public building. The woman's lined face spoke of years of laughter and tears, sun and hard work. As usual, Slider knew how to choose his subject.

There was no real reason why the small group could not wait in the cushioned chairs of the city council meeting room. After all, it was their city hall, too. April felt embarrassed anger as she realized the minority representatives did not feel welcome inside. Then a gentle breeze teased at the short hair on the back of her neck. It felt good. The hint of a sunset cast a rosy glow on the plain brick fronts of the downtown buildings. April decided that waiting outside wasn't such a bad idea.

A glance at her watch reminded April that the city council meeting would start soon. She wanted to take her place at the media table and exchange greetings with the mayor and council members. It wasn't her first visit to Angusville. They knew her, and she them. April found them, as a whole, to be a decent group, despite their lack of awareness as an empowered body of all white males. April felt insensitivity was their greatest crime. She sighed as she glanced over her shoulder at the quiet group of Hispanic constituents. As a practiced observer of the political process, April doubted they would be particularly effective in improving the awareness of their city council.

Slider snapped his last picture and stepped to April's side. He too was aware of the importance of arriving early. They'd just opened the glass door and stepped inside, when a car pulled into the parking lot. A tall, Hispanic woman, dressed in a gray jacket and skirt, and carrying a leather briefcase, stepped from the car. The group of protesters called cheery greetings, and April noted the glow of their faces as they circled the new arrival. April smiled. She appreciated these new developments. Before the evening was over, she predicted an improvement in the city council's social consciousness.

"Hey! What's the holdup?" Slider hissed at his co-worker from where he stood, holding the council chamber door. April trotted down the hall and entered the meeting room just in front of Slider.

"Well, this is a fine surprise," said Tom Thurmond, the mayor, as he spotted the city journalists. The gray hair and thickening waist of the aging gentleman did little to hide the handsome charm of his youth. "To what do we owe this visit?" he asked.

"Just making our rounds," April lied. Mayor Thurmond knew she was lying, and April knew that the mayor knew. They smiled graciously at each other. It was all part of the game.

April took her seat at the media table, next to a quiet man with the hesitant look of the young and inexperienced. She had heard that the *Angusville Brand* had hired a new reporter. Like many small-town papers, they went through freshly graduated students like teenagers through hamburgers. Only those handicapped by lack of experience would tolerate the poverty-level wages of a small-town reporter. She smiled encouragement at the young man, exchanging names and handshakes as Slider snapped a few quick shots of the councilmen seated at the half-circle table. Once the meeting started, photos were forbidden.

Thirty folding chairs rested in neat rows before the council table. There would have been thirty empty chairs without the presence of one gentleman whose expensive, three-piece suit looked more like it should be seated on leather rather than the cold, gray paint of low-bid public property. April glanced at the agenda and noted the scheduled presence of an architect. The three-piece suit now made sense.

With a hesitant push, the Hispanic man who had studied April's press card opened the chamber door and led his tiny contingent to sit on the cold metal of the two back rows. April turned her attention to the group. Her gaze never progressed beyond the tall, dark-haired woman with the clothing and bearing of a professional and the flashing dark eyes of a Latina.

April's mind locked down. If it were her computer, she could hit the reset button and get things back online. Her brain did not have a reset button. Instead, her eyes moved on their very own to stare at the woman's soft, black hair and trace the shape of a strong face with soft lines. Finally, her gaze rested, with no desire to move further, on the length of shapely legs beneath the woman's gray skirt.

The meeting started, but April continued to stare, not hearing the drone of the mayor's voice as he opened the session. She did not hear the reading of the minutes, nor did she notice the questioning glances from the young reporter at her side. Before the situation progressed to embarrassing, Slider jerked his partner back to reality with a resounding thump to the back of her head. The young journalist stared at Slider, his eyes wide with surprise.

"It's part of a photographer's job to wake up the reporter when she goes to sleep," Slider whispered in his ear. The young man nodded, not really understanding.

April blushed a bright red and forced her attention back to the meeting just as the city council voted to accept the monthly budget report. Everything seemed routine. April closed her eyes and gave her brain the equivalent of a mental cold shower. There was work to do. The length and shape of any participant's legs had nothing to do with the council meeting she must cover. She glanced at the agenda and realized that Slider's helpful thump had come none too soon. It was time to go to work. She punched the record button on her digital recorder and pushed it to the edge of the table.

"I'm sure all of the members of the city council are as thrilled as I am about the outcome of our recent bond issue," Mayor Thurmond said, as he opened discussion on the first agenda item. "I am extremely pleased the voters chose to support our proposition, despite the increase in property taxes."

"We cannot hope to attract businesses of any size to our city without a community athletics center," agreed Don Ferrell, a banker who rarely visited much of the community beyond his own office, his favorite Mexican restaurant, and the country club. He was well aware of the role racquetball played in the modern business world.

A wry smile played at the corners of the lined and weathered mouth of Thad James. He had moved within Angusville city limits ten years earlier, but he was, and always would be, a rancher—a country man with straightforward ways and a quiet passion for justice.

"I'm sure you're right about that Don, but I'm

just glad our youngsters will have something to do on Saturday night besides driving up and down Main Street and parking at the lake." Thad looked beyond his fellow councilmen and toward the Hispanic contingent. "Manuel, I'm sorry if these property taxes are going to cause you folks problems."

The man who had studied April's press card stood hesitantly. "*Señor* James, as I told you, many of us cannot pay higher taxes and hope to keep our homes."

The rancher's lips tightened and his eyes softened with a mild sorrow. "I know, Manuel, but I don't know what we can do. Mayor Thurmond and I discussed it with the city attorney. It seems that it's just not possible for us to make an exception for one small section of town. You all out in the San Juan community already have the lowest property evaluations around."

"I don't mean to be callous, but, as a banker, I feel that someone who cannot afford the taxes should not own property." Don Ferrell interrupted. "Perhaps you could check on some of the new HUD housing that's available for low rent."

April made a quick note to check on who provided the financing for the low-cost (and poorly built) housing intended primarily for migrant farm workers. This was not the first rat she'd smelled in Don Ferrell's presence.

"Excuse me. May I speak?"

April's mouth went dry. The dark-haired woman's voice was as lovely and as smooth as April would have hoped in the fantasy she was already building around this unknown stranger. April focused on her notepad for the simple reason that she did not dare look at the dark-haired Latina. She feared her infatuation would run away with her mind once again, leaving her unable to listen and function.

Mayor Thurmond leaned forward and looked closely at the Hispanic professional. "Sophia Mendez, is that you?"

"Yes, Mayor Thurmond. It is."

"Why young lady, I haven't seen you for ten years. See your father now and again, and he's kept me up to date. I understand you're practicing law in Amber now."

"Yes, sir. I am," the golden voice answered.

"We're pleased to have you back in Angusville, even if it's just for a visit," the mayor said.

April studied the mayor's face. She could see the cogs turning as he calculated the political risk posed by the unexpected visitor, but she could see also that he meant his words. There was a hint of pride as he looked at the tall Latina.

"And what might your business be here tonight?" asked Don Ferrell, not trying to hide his impatience.

"Gentleman, I'm very concerned about the matter of continued taxation of property in the San Juan community," she responded.

"Miss Mendez, if you can suggest a solution, I'd be more than happy to hear it," Councilman James said, a flicker of hope in his eyes.

"At Mr. Garcia's request I looked into San Juan taxation, and I found that your city attorney is correct. As a city council, you cannot opt to exempt this one community from increased ad valorem taxes."

Councilman James sighed and ran his fingers through thinning hair. "That's not what I wanted to hear."

"I was surprised to find that San Juan was never

officially incorporated into the city of Angusville," the dark-haired woman continued.

April watched the council closely, evaluating reactions. Councilman James looked confused, Councilman Ferrell irritated, and there was a flash of understanding in the mayor's eyes. A silence grew as the lawyer waited for the council to respond to her statement.

"Of course not," Ferrell said. "There's not a prayer that the residents of San Juan could improve their property to meet the city codes for sewers, paving, and structural quality. We'd have to condemn half their homes."

The long-legged lawyer pulled a file from her briefcase and looked inside. April strongly suspected that the woman didn't need to refresh her memory so much as she wanted the council to know that she had certain documents in her possession.

"The area is not incorporated, and yet the city of Angusville has collected ad valorem taxes from San Juan residents for the past thirty-three years," Sophia Mendez said.

April heard a soft chuckle from Councilman James as the light dawned. Despite his practiced cool, a twinkle deepened the blue of Mayor Thurmond's eyes.

"Of course we've collected taxes. The community's right on our doorstep," Ferrell whined.

April forgot her resolve not to look at the woman. The reporter glanced up in time to see a flash of fire in deep-brown eyes.

"Councilman Ferrell, the city collected those taxes illegally." She motioned with the folder in her hands. "I have prepared the documents necessary to file suit for repayment of those unlawful public revenues."

The mayor cleared his throat. It was time for the master politician to take command.

"I do not believe that will be necessary, Miss Mendez," the mayor said.

"I certainly hope not, Mayor Thurmond."

Councilman Ferrell started to speak, but was silenced by a stone-cold stare from Councilman James. Besides the respect demanded by the hardened physical presence of the outdoorsman, April also suspected that the rancher's sizable real estate holdings made him one of Ferrell's largest depositors.

"May I suggest that you set up an appointment with the city attorney to discuss an equitable means of resolving this problem?" the mayor continued.

"That sounds reasonable," the attorney answered.

"Miss Mendez, we really appreciate you coming to help us out in this matter," Councilman James said.

"I only seek to serve my clients," she responded. She returned the documents to the briefcase in the chair beside her. "If you gentlemen will excuse me, I have a long drive back to Amber."

As the woman gathered her belongings and exited from the chamber, followed by the small group of protesters, April half stood, unable to fully fight the urge to follow. Once again, Slider was there for her. He grasped her by the elbow and pulled her to her chair.

"Don't sweat it." He tapped the notepad before her. "You've got her name, and how many Hispanic female attorneys can there be in Amber?"

April knew he was right. Still, as she heard the murmur of voices through the closed chamber doors, she felt a sick sense of lost opportunity.

❧ ❧ ❧ ❧

Sophia Mendez accepted gratefully the warm hugs and gentle words from the people of the San Juan community. It was good to be home, at least for a short time. Her father, one of the more affluent Hispanics in the community, waited for her at his home…the house that had been her home throughout her childhood until she married. Even then, she and her husband had lived in the small house across the road, one her father bought for the young couple. Everyone in Angusville knew her father, Tomás Mendez. The man, or one of his mechanics, kept every car in town on the road. Whether it was replacing transmissions or installing new tires, the townspeople knew Mendez Auto Shop as reliable, honest, and affordable.

Her parents had supported her choices to a point, but Sophia was still a Hispanic woman. Her lust for knowledge could not totally override cultural expectations. She married her high school boyfriend, son of another respected Hispanic family, more a result of her mother's expectations than out of any real love or commitment to her husband. It had been a brief and tumultuous marriage. Sophia turned down a scholarship to UT Austin, because her husband refused to move while she went to college. Both families felt it was more important that he stay to learn the trade in his own father's flooring and upholstery business. Instead, she accepted a scholarship to the nearby West Texas A&M and commuted to classes. She did not bother to tell her mother about her studies in pre-law, letting her mother believe she simply planned to return to Angusville as a teacher. She never had to actually lie. Her mother created her own reality. Simple silence enabled her to keep those illusions.

The divorce was inevitable. As she pursued her studies, her young husband never gave up his nights out with former classmates. When a young girl, still a junior in high school, turned up pregnant and claimed Sophia's husband as the father, Sophia secretly breathed a sigh of relief. Neither her mother, nor even the local priest, could deny her filing for her legal freedom. Although he never said so, Sophia was sure her father knew the truth. After all, when her ex-husband was free to marry again, he did, giving a legitimate name to the child he sired and to the three others who followed. He and his wife and children still lived in the house Sophia had once shared with him, and her parents claimed their children as grandchildren. Sophia secretly enjoyed watching the growing and loving family, and the children called her *Tia* Sophia.

Her father lived alone. Breast cancer had taken her mother. Sophia had taken a semester away from law school to care for her dying mother. She remembered those final days as bittersweet, as mother accepted daughter not as she wanted her to be, but as she was. No matter how many years passed, Sophia always felt the sting of tears when she remembered the day her weakened mother had taken her hand and pulled her close, touching Sophia's face gently.

"I am so proud of you, *Hita,*" the dying woman said, a profound peace reflected in her eyes. "You finish school, my daughter. I am glad your dreams were bigger than the ones I had for you."

Sophia kissed her mother on the forehead. "Do

you think you could eat some soup today, *Madre*?"

Her mother nodded, and Sophia went to the kitchen to heat the homemade *caldo de pollo*. When she returned, her mother slept peacefully. Sophia woke her gently, and the woman was able to eat and enjoy much of the simple food.

Whenever she came home, Sophia always remembered that day and the sweet comfort it gave her. Her mother had died within a month, and in many ways, that had been their shared moment of farewell.

As she reminisced, Sophia barely heard the words of the people of San Juan. She gently shook her head, bringing herself back to the present.

The crowd of well-wishers began to disperse, and she turned to Manuel Garcia, the man whose request for help had brought her home for this council meeting.

"Manuel, there were three people I did not know in the council chambers, a woman, a man and a younger man,"

"That would be the people from the newspapers," Manuel answered.

"Newspapers?"

"Yes, the boy is from the *Angusville Brand*, and the others were from the city paper."

"The *Amber Daily*?" Sophia asked.

"*Sí.*" Manuel pulled a business card April had given him from his pocket and handed it to Sophia.

Sophia looked at the card, recognizing the name from many bylines she had seen in the newspaper. She was relieved. Now that she recognized the reporter and her work, she felt certain the meeting would be covered without bias. Besides, she had liked the looks of the woman. Sophia allowed herself a moment of longing. She worked with men in a man's world day after day. Sometimes she longed for a female friend, but she never felt totally comfortable with the legal and administrative assistants in the office when she joined them for lunch. The conversation always turned to one man or another…perhaps one woman expressing frustration with her husband, or single women talking of the men they wanted to date. Sophia could only listen, nodding encouragement. Her desire to tie herself to any man evaporated with her divorce. Occasional and sometimes passionate short-term relationships reminded her that she was truly a woman, but the experience always left her with an ill-defined hunger.

Sophia longed for a woman friend who could be her peer, one who shared her commitment to serve the greater good, as well as her lack of desire for husband and children. She looked at the name on the card again. The woman behind the articles she read had a great sense of commitment and courage. *Could she be the friend I need, the one who would listen to my thoughts and desires and truly understand?*

The card went directly into her suit jacket pocket. For the moment, it was forgotten.

Chapter Four

April sipped repeatedly at a rapidly emptying soda can. It didn't help. Her mouth still felt dry as cotton. In contrast, a damp film covered her palms, giving an unpleasant, slick feel to the polished aluminum of the can.

"Calm down," Johnnie ordered as she threw a paper tablecloth over one of the ratty tables in one corner of the Ladies' Room. "You'd think you were getting married or something."

April placed her soda on the counter and wiped both hands on her jeans. It didn't help. The palms remained sweaty.

"I'm just scared nobody'll show up."

"So, what am I? Chopped liver?" Johnnie asked.

"You know what I mean. If just you and the guys from the Diamonds show up, then we might as well have met at my house."

Johnnie neatly arranged paper plates, cups, and a pitcher of iced tea on the table. "Chill, honey. If all we do is shoot the bull in a new place, then we'll have a good time just like we always do. No harm in that."

A haunted look gave April's eyes the pitiful gleam of a chastised puppy. "Johnnie, I really, really want this to work."

Johnnie placed a hand on her friend's arm. "I know, honey, but if it doesn't fly tonight, that don't mean the idea is dead. You'll just have to wait a little longer."

"And work a little harder."

"Maybe some of that, too."

Mo appeared at the doorway, bearing the bag of chips she'd promised. Billboard and Allison trailed behind. Billboard carried a container of French onion dip to go with Mo's chips, and Allison held a pan of home-baked brownies.

"Hey Allison. How'd you get those brownies out of the house without the kids stealing any?" Johnnie asked.

"I made two pans," the mother answered. "Bubba and Morrie are at home happily ruining their dinner."

"Sounds like a good idea to me," Billboard said, as she took the first brownie from the pan even before Allison could rest it on the table.

"You guys know if anyone else is coming?" April asked.

Mo laughed. "Relax, girl. People know about our meeting. Your fliers are in both bars, and I saw your little notice in the paper."

"I can't believe you did that," Allison observed.

"What's the problem?" Johnnie defended her friend. "If readers don't know what she's talking about, they'd never know what she's talking about."

Billboard grinned and quoted, "'All Lambda Ladies interested in 'family' issues are invited to attend a discussion group in the newly opened Ladies' Room above the Pink Triangle at Tenth and Seymour on Tuesday night at 8 p.m.'"

"Am I discreet or what?" April asked.

"I just hope you weren't so discreet that we get some sorority sisters thinking we're going to talk about raising children," Mo said.

April's face turned a new shade of pale. Johnnie punched her friend on the arm.

"Don't worry! If we end up with some socialites, we'll just feed them brownies and educate them on a few subjects they most likely never discuss in their other women's clubs."

Billboard rummaged through the cooler. "Hey, where's the beer?"

"You want a beer, you can go down to the bar." April answered.

Billboard looked up, surprised. She raised both hands in a gesture of surrender. "No sweat. Sorry, I just didn't know the ground rules."

"I guess we can smoke?" Mo asked, as she searched beneath the cabinets for something to use as an ashtray.

"Only if you sit by the door," her sister answered.

Mo raised her eyebrows and looked to April.

"Sounds like a good rule to me," April responded.

Billboard opened a can of Coke and then stretched across half of one couch. She was silent, and her lips drew into a sullen frown. Mo grabbed a chair and sat far from the group, blowing smoke through the open doorway. The room filled with silence. A tension grew around April's heart. The first meeting of the Ladies' Room had not even begun, and two women already felt alienated. April looked at Mo and Billboard, wondering how she could heal the rift.

"Guys, listen. I'm sorry about the beer and the smoking, but Tandy and I talked long and hard about what we want the Ladies' Room to do."

"And what about what we want?" Mo asked from her distant seat.

April chewed at her lower lip. Searching for

inspiration. "Billboard, some women don't go to the bars because they can't handle the alcohol or they hate the way others act when they drink."

"That's not the same as just having a beer," Billboard answered.

April secretly wondered. She tried to remember the last time Billboard failed to bring a cooler of beer to a ball game.

"Yeah, maybe so," April answered, "but if somebody who hated the bars walked in here and saw us sipping on longnecks, what do you suppose she'd think?"

Billboard looked inside her Coke can, apparently searching the dark fluid for an answer. "I guess she'd think we were just another part of the Pink Triangle."

"That's my point."

Allison leaned over the back of the couch and pointed an accusing finger at her sister. "And you, Morley Ann Thompson. You should've quit smoking years ago."

With exaggerated movements, Johnnie stashed her pack of Salem Lights under her t-shirt. "Don't guess I'll be lighting up tonight," the first base woman said.

"Get off my back, Alli," Mo responded as she guiltily snuffed her cigarette in a jar. "You know I've tried to quit."

"Then you need to try harder," her sister responded.

"It's my body and my health. Leave me alone!" Mo argued.

Tears appeared in Allison's eyes. "Damn it! It's tough to watch someone I love smoking their way into an early grave." She raised her head, pausing to consider her next words. "Like we did, Dad."

Mo jerked. April could swear she saw a red handprint on the side of Mo's face. Obviously Allison's comment had hit home. April, Johnnie, and Billboard listened in silence. They all had shared shifts sitting with the two sisters in cold, hospital waiting rooms during the final days of their father's battle with lung cancer.

"Alli, I've really tried to quit," Mo almost whispered.

"Did I tell you I caught Bubba out in the garage smoking one of your cigarettes?" Alli whispered in return.

Mo's tightened face looked even more stricken. She looked at the half-full pack of cigarettes in her hand and then absently tossed them into a nearby trashcan.

"I guess I'll try again," she said.

Allison lumbered out of her seat and crossed the room to give her sister a bear hug that made the coach's bones pop so loud the other women could hear from across the room. Everyone watched in silence, enjoying the warmth of the moment and secretly embarrassed by its intensity.

"Looks like a special 'family' moment to me, and I mean 'family' both ways," Johnnie finally said.

The hesitant thump of footsteps on the exterior stairs interrupted the laughter. April inched forward, barely holding her seat as she willed the unseeing visitors into the room.

"Hey, come on in," Mo called as the new arrivals reached the top of the stairs.

Three women appeared in the doorway. One woman, a copy of April's flier in her hand, walked boldly inside. She moved well within the room, leaving ample space for the other two women to enter around her sizeable form.

"We got the right place?" she asked in a voice easily heard by anyone with hearing this side of total deafness. "We're a bunch of Lambda Ladies looking for a place to light." The woman squared her shoulders and stood tall, showing more clearly the dinner-plate sized beltbuckle that said "XIT Rodeo and Reunion, All-Around Cowgirl, 1996."

"Come inside," Mo said to the two other women who still stood hesitantly outside the door. "We don't bite."

"Damn. Maybe we do have the wrong place," All-Around Cowgirl said. "I might go for a little biting."

"Sorry, honey. We left the whips and chains at home, too," Johnnie responded.

"But we got homemade brownies," April added.

The big woman's boots clomped across the floor, as she walked to the table and studied the food and drink. "Not bad for a Tuesday night, I guess."

One of the new arrivals walked to All-Around Cowgirl's side and placed a hand on the big woman's arm. "Sandy, mind your manners," she said.

"It's okay, Stella, honey. These folks don't mind a big country girl like me, do y'all?"

April smiled and called her welcome along with the rest of the Diamonds. Truth was, April had rapidly achieved a liking for this gregarious cowgirl.

"We're glad you could come," April said. "I guess you know this is the first meeting of the Ladies' Room Discussion Group."

"Nope, all we knew was we'd never heard of it before."

Johnnie helped April rearrange chairs so that the three arrivals could take seats in the circle. "My name's April, and Tandy…I guess you know Tandy, don't you? You know…the owner of the Pink Triangle."

All-Around Cowgirl laughed. "I think I once met a *caballero* from Juarez that didn't know her, but that's the only one. If you're queer in Texas, you know Tandy. If you don't, you're either not queer or you ain't in Texas."

"Sandy!" All-Around Cowgirl's lover groaned. "Honey, sometimes you talk too much."

The cowgirl, holding a plate filled with chips and brownies, took a seat beside her lover. "Scuse me, folks. Sometimes I forget myself. By the way, my name's Sandy and this here's my lady, Stella." She motioned toward the third new arrival. The woman, as tiny and rail thin as Sandy was tall and stout, had taken a hesitant seat on an end of a couch nearest her two friends. "This bag of skin and bones is our friend, Judy. She works out at the Four Sixes, near Boomer, and don't make it to town much."

April had heard of the ranch, and she admired the woman's courage for living the solitary life of a cowhand. Everything about her told the story of Judy's daily existence. Her face and hands were weathered and tanned, giving the blue of her eyes an added depth. "Sungrins" lined her eyes, making it almost impossible to guess the woman's age.

"I live out at East Camp," the woman added in a clear, soft voice.

"Don't them nasty old cowboys bother you?" Johnnie asked.

The blue of her eyes took on a devilish gleam. "No. They've seen me shoot," she answered. The group laughed a warm response.

No one heard, as a young girl slipped through the door and took a seat just outside the group. Johnnie noticed her presence and smiled a welcome as she subtly motioned to April, pointing out the new arrival. April looked at her watch.

"Anyway, as I was telling Sandy earlier, Tandy asked me to sort of head up the Ladies' Room Discussion Group, and it's eight twenty. I guess according to Gay Standard Time that means it's time to start."

April relaxed as everyone gave their name and told something about themselves. Most mentioned the work they did or where they lived. April could barely hear the quiet girl in the back. Her something about herself was a mumbled, "I'm new to all this." April smiled so hard, willing warmth toward the girl, that her face hurt. It took two tries before the girl spoke up enough that the group could hear her give Terry as her name.

An awkward silenced followed the introductions. The sound of cowgirl Sandy munching tortilla chips echoed off the walls, and every woman in the room turned to watch her eat.

"Hey, I didn't know I was going to be the evening's entertainment," Sandy said, as she wiped tortilla crumbs from her mouth.

Laughter eased the silence, but it returned like water rushing into a gaping hole in the side of a boat. Everyone turned to April, waiting for her to set a new direction. Deep inside her head, April released a silent groan from the weight of their expectations.

"Since this is the very first session of the Ladies' Room Discussion Group, I'm not real sure how we're going to proceed," April said.

"Honey, you know more than you let on," Johnnie interrupted. She reached for the notebook at April's side and raised it for all to see. "She's been thinking up subjects for this here discussion group to discuss for over three weeks. When we get rolling, it won't be boring. I even saw her writing questions about religion and politics."

"Religion and politics!!" Mo moaned in mock agony. "First, you women make me give up my cigarettes and now you want me to talk about religion and politics."

April glared at Johnnie. "I was debating whether or not we should get into any serious topics tonight. For the first meeting, I just wanted us all to get to know each other."

Billboard stopped etching designs with her thumbnail in her Coke can and turned to Mo. "What you got against discussing religion and politics?"

"Nothing, as long as everybody agrees with me."

Sandy laughed. "At least she's honest."

"Seems to me, we all need to be a little more concerned about politics than we are," Stella said. Everyone turned in surprise to Sandy's lover. It was the first she'd spoken since telling everybody she worked in the Moore County Clerk's Office. She was soft-spoken compared to her gregarious lover, but her voice was clear and easy to hear. April thought the clarity of her words matched the deep directness of her gaze.

"What you mean?" Billboard asked.

"I guess you guys know about the sodomy law," Stella said.

"Yeah, it's a real bitch for the guys," Mo responded. "It's just not fair that the state of Texas should tell them what they can do in their own bedroom."

"Guys, smuys," Johnnie taunted. "The sodomy law applies to all us homosexual deviants."

"You're kidding," Mo said. "But sodomy…"

"In this case is a legal term to apply to all forms of homosexuality," April finished.

"Shit." Billboard commented. "You mean, we could go to jail?"

"That's the way I understand it," April said.

"I've never heard of it being enforced around here, but they could," Johnnie added. "It would be interesting to hear what an attorney has to say."

The word attorney triggered an automatic response between Stella and Sandy. Their eyes locked in a shared concern, and Sandy rested her plate on her lap, turning her full attention to the subject at hand.

"Any of you fella's know a good attorney?" Sandy asked.

"I've met a few through my work at the newspaper, but most of them are criminal attorneys," April answered. Her brows creased, and she was surprised at the comfortable warmth of the thought as she remembered Sophia Mendez. "I did meet one the other day, but I don't know much about her."

"Her?" Johnnie's voice held a curious edge.

"Yeah, her. Women can be attorneys too, you know."

"I'd sure like to talk to a woman attorney," Sandy commented.

Stella cleared her throat and looked at the faces around her. The woman appeared to be making a judgement about the safety of the space in which she found herself. April was gratified when she decided to continue.

"I'm supposed to have surgery next month," Stella said. "Nothing too serious, a hysterectomy actually, but I'd like to make sure the hospital knows that Sandy's the one I want making any decisions and not my family."

Sandy nervously crumbled a chip to dust in her plate. "The whole thing's got us to talking about wills and such, too. We've been together fifteen years, and I'd sure hate for my asshole brother to try to take the house away from Stella if anything happened to me."

"Shoot, I can understand that," Allison said. "I never thought about gay couples needing extra legal papers just to say they really are a couple."

April smiled at a new thought. "Tell you what. I'll get in touch with this lady attorney, and maybe she'll come talk to us during the next meeting."

General murmurs of approval informed April that she had stumbled on a successful game plan. She was beginning to feel good about the evening.

"Can we talk about religion now?" a quiet voice asked from the back of the room. All eyes turned to Terry, the quiet girl who had managed to find a chair that wasn't entirely in the open circle. April's heart fell to her knees as she saw the tears in the young woman's eyes.

"Sure, honey. We can talk about anything you want," Johnnie answered for the group.

Tears streamed down Terry's face in earnest. "I...I don't know..." Her voice shook as she tried to continue.

"You just take your time. We're all here to listen," Mo encouraged.

"My family...threw me out."

"Because you're gay?" April asked softly.

Terry nodded and mouthed the yes that she didn't have the heart to say.

"Damnation! And they call that family values," Sandy grumbled.

Johnnie left her seat on the couch and pulled a chair close to the trembling girl. She put her arm over delicate shoulders, and Terry leaned her face against the older woman's shoulder, welcoming the comfort she found there.

"You listen to me, girl," Johnnie said in a voice gruff with kindness. "You're family, they made a serious mistake thinking that you're not good enough to be a part of them, just because you were made to love women instead of men. Don't you make that same mistake. You're a fine young woman, and now you're free to choose your own family, one that will appreciate you for you, not for what they want you to be."

Terry leaned away, shaking her head in mild protest as she took the box of tissues Stella offered.

"They didn't want to kick me out," she mumbled. Her voice took on a new edge, tinged slightly with a tone of hate. "He told them they had to."

Every woman leaned closer, waiting to learn who he might be.

"Who made them?" April asked.

"The preacher," Terry's voice dripped venom. Silence filled the vacuum as the women waited for the girl to continue. She tore at a tissue, converting its damp mass to a wad of sodden bits in her lap.

"I wouldn't deny what I felt for Marilyn," Terry continued, her voice barely above a whisper. The stilled concentration in the room was such that no one had difficulty hearing her softened words. "The preacher told my family they had to denounce me or be doomed to hell, so they threw me out. Mamma cried like there wasn't going to be a tomorrow, and my brother slipped me two hundred dollars, all the money he had in the world, but they did what the preacher said."

April studied the woman, little more than a child really. "How old are you, Terry?" she asked.

"Just turned seventeen."

April could almost hear the word jailbait as it rumbled through Johnnie's mind, and she directed a scathing look at her friend as a precaution against any temptation Johnnie might have to verbalize that thought. Johnnie raised one eyebrow, acknowledging the nonverbal message.

"That must have been awful for you, honey. How have you been living?" Stella asked.

"I have a cousin that took me in. I've been working in her husband's grocery store as a stocker, and he even lets me off to go to school. It's not so bad…except…except…"

"Except what?" Allison asked.

New tears flowed down Terry's cheeks. These were different tears, deeper tears, tears from a hurt that might scar and harden, but would never fully heal.

"Except for…Marilyn." She looked at her hands, not even noticing the silent tears that dropped from her face to those hands folded in false serenity. "She …she denied our love, and the preacher told her family they had to move away to get her away from my devilish ways. They moved back to the family farm near Fort Morgan, and that's the last I heard from her."

Johnnie stroked the child's hair. "Don't feel

she betrayed you. She just did what she had to do to survive."

Terry's shoulders shook in silent sobs. The intensity of her grief tightened every throat in the room. April felt tears building in her own eyes.

"No…she didn't," Terry said. No one else spoke. No words could ease the pain they saw. "They…they found her in the closet." Terry's hands remained calm and folded in her lap. "She used her father's belt…the one he used to beat her."

For a moment April sat, confused by the young girl's explanation. As realization dawned, she glanced at the faces around her and watched horror flash across their features like a wave in the crowd at a baseball game.

"When did she hang herself?" April asked gently, but with the reporter's need to clarify the obvious.

Terry looked directly at her, and April felt caught in the whirlpool of grief reflected in the younger woman's eyes.

"Four months ago," Terry answered. The calmly folded hands began to shake, and a wail of pain erupted from her tiny form. Johnnie threw her arms around the child, and the girl collapsed in the comfort, for the first time expressing freely the grief she had held alone for so long. Stella, crossed the room and added her touch to the simple, physical comfort Johnnie offered.

"You can be sure that Marilyn's at peace now," Johnnie said.

"And she never stopped loving you," Stella added.

A roomful of women watched a young girl grieve. Without exception, everyone, even those who could not offer simple touch, willed her their strength and healing. Somewhere among the shared tears and common goal, a bond was built. The Ladies' Room had its beginning.

⚘ ⚘ ⚘ ⚘

"I was sure glad that Stella and Sandy knew that counselor," Mo said, as she folded the paper cloth covering the rickety wooden table.

"We were lucky," April said. "Sure let me know that we need to start building a resource list."

"Sounds like you've already lined up an attorney," Johnnie said. April looked at her, wondering at the hint of hostility in her friend's voice.

April, Mo, Johnnie, and Allison continued to clean up from the first meeting of the Ladies' Room Discussion Group. It would take longer to sort through the mess the evening had left within their hearts and minds.

"Lord, I hope that girl's gonna' be okay," Mo said.

"She'll survive, and maybe we can help her some," Allison responded.

"By the way, did any of you all catch who the preacher was who caused all the trouble with Terry?" Johnnie asked.

April's brows creased as she tried to remember. "Did she mention a name?"

"Not to the group, but she told me when we were talking, before Sandy, Stella, and Judy offered to take her home."

"Who is he?" April asked.

Johnnie placed her hands on her hips and wagged her head in a defiant gesture. "None other than Reverend Ralph Thomas, the same holy roller who's been writing high sounding letters to the editor about all us homosexuals being of the devil and such stuff."

Mo shook her head. "How can someone say he's a man of God and preach nothing but hate?"

A tap at the open doorway interrupted the conversation. The four women looked up to see two new arrivals. April's mouth dropped open as she spied the two women, both dressed in the latest fashions, and each with matching purse and pumps. It brought back memories of her mother and Easter Sunday.

"I'm sorry we're so late," one woman said. "But our regular Lakeview Study Club meeting was tonight." She looked at the jeans and t-shirts of the Lambda Ladies and then studied the ragged humbleness of the room. "Are we in the right place? We understood a sorority was hosting a seminar about family issues."

The laughter started with Johnnie and soon invaded all four friends. With great self-control April stopped laughing long enough to offer the newcomers a seat, a soda, and a very entertaining explanation.

Chapter Five

The tune April whistled sounded like a cross between Jim Morrison and an Antioch Baptist spiritual. The mixture created music with little form or meaning, but it certainly was cheerful.

Sam Trimble poked his head through the door of his office and glared into the newsroom. "Jesus Christ. Would somebody shoot whatever poor animal is making that pitiful noise and put it out of its misery?" he huffed.

April's mouth froze in mid-whistle, as she realized he referred to her melody. She didn't look up from the computer screen as she continued to type the details of a routine story. "Sorry, Boss. Just felt so good that I didn't even realize I was whistling."

"Whistling. Is that what you call it? I thought you were practicing sound effects for a horror movie," Sam huffed. He walked to her desk and stood hunched with his hands on his hips. April recognized her boss's well-disguised attempt at friendliness. The attention of his friendliness had been known to send junior reporters weeping into the streets. It had been many years since April was tempted to run crying from the newsroom, but her acerbic editor did encourage April into frequent bouts of swearing in the dark room. Slider knew how to listen in relative silence with only mild amusement. April didn't really mind. Sam was one hell of an editor. Lack of personality proved only a minor liability.

Sam continued to glare at his star reporter with the infrequent facial expression that those who knew him learned to associate with either a smile or indigestion. April gave up on her story and turned her attention to her boss.

"What's up Mr. Sam?"

Sam stuck his hands in his suspenders and plopped into the wobbly, wooden chair April kept for those subjects who were foolish enough to come to the newsroom for an interview. April hated in-office interviews. It took years to fully develop the ability to concentrate in the midst of mayhem. The hunted expressions that soon developed on the faces of hapless visitors were a warning sign to April. She knew that the quotes would be poor and the subject at hand poorly covered. In the newsroom, the person being interviewed fought with distractions all around. The verbal battle between a society reporter and a sports writer over the last jelly doughnut sounded like a potential bloodletting. Then there was always the ever-popular, uninvited tirade from a public official, unhappy with the fact that the paper had dared report on his hand caught in the cookie jar. It mattered little that he had been caught with his hand, arm, and entire right shoulder completely covered in snicker doodles. These visits were especially distracting for the interview subject, since April was usually the recipient of these heated monologues. After all, April's job included keeping track of the cookie levels in local coffers. She took her job seriously, so much so that there were now three notches carved on the bottom edge of the center drawer of her desk. Each notch stood for a death threat, a sure sign of a successful investigative reporter. Two more and she would contest the record of Sam Trimble himself.

"I read the feature you wrote on minority accomplishments in the city," Sam said, pulling April's mind back to the present.

April held her breath, waiting for the ax to fall. Sam had left his office to talk to her about a story. Her mind raced, trying to remember some obvious detail she could have overlooked.

"And?" she asked.

"And…" Sam scratched at a patch of gravy drying on the front of his shirt. "…I liked it," he said.

"What?" April asked, astonished.

"I think we've got our feature entry for the annual Texas Associated Press competition," he added.

Sam hauled his sizable frame out of the creaking chair and stood to tower over her. He pointed a stern finger at the veteran reporter. "Don't let it go to your head. Hear me?"

"Wouldn't think of it." April said, her mouth still open in shock.

"Besides, you still use too damn many adjectives." Sam gave a parting shot before he stomped back to the inner sanctum of his office.

A semi-hush had fallen over the newsroom. Actual quiet was reserved for the end of the world. The fishbowl aspect of the newsroom encouraged the free sharing of information from desk to desk. The huge, open room also encouraged the free flow of gossip. Little was missed in a room full of people whose entire professional life focused on looking for the details. Unfortunately, the habit spilled over into personal lives as well.

The entire newsroom saw Sam Trimble leave

his office. The entire newsroom saw him sit at April's desk and carry on a conversation. No one knew what had been said in that conversation. The second-year reporter, four desks down, was already composing a letter to persuade Sam to give him the senior reporter's job following April's termination. An apprentice photographer had scurried to the nether world of the darkroom in a search for Slider, thinking April might be in need of her friend's support. The sports section had already begun a pool, betting whether or not the dyke on the news desk was finally getting canned for being queer. No one…nary a soul would have predicted that Sam's heart to heart with the senior reporter had actually been an opportunity for the managing editor to complement a story. Within minutes, rumors crossed the news section, flitted through society, and wandered back to the city editor's private office, three doors down from Sam Trimble's.

Kate Stevens erupted from her office like a race horse out of the gate. Her eyes blazed as she strode toward April's desk, where April still sat with her mouth open, a fixed gaze directed toward the now-closed door to Sam Trimble's office.

"What's that old warhorse think he's doing?" Kate demanded. "If he's got a problem with your work, he knows he should come to me first," the city editor continued, a harsh edge to her voice.

April's mouth closed and a smile covered her face. Her good fortune was beginning to feel like reality. First, the managing editor likes her work, and now the city editor is ready to do battle for her.

"Chill out, Kate," April answered. "You're not going to believe it."

"What?" Kate straightened her dress before

she sat. The woman maintained a dignity in both her appearance and her thinking that April had always respected. She maintained that hard shell so common in the world of journalism, but, in the years they'd known each other, April had been allowed to see the warm and gentle woman inside.

"Sam just wanted to tell me he liked the feature about minority accomplishments," April said.

"You're kidding."

"No, honest to God."

Kate sat in the same rickety chair Sam had occupied. It didn't creak nearly as bad nor fill nearly as completely as it had with Sam. Kate thought for a moment and then chuckled.

"Lord, it takes him a long time to think on things. Old fart should have noticed what an ace you are years ago."

What could have been a glow of pleasure was only a mild blush on April's face. She cautioned herself to be careful. If one cared too much about an editor's compliments, it could make the criticism that was sure to come totally devastating.

"Thanks, Kate. That means a lot coming from you."

A devilish smile creased the wrinkles around the older woman's eyes. "Now, that means you'll just have to work all the harder to do better."

April groaned and laid her head on her desk. "Does it never end?"

Kate stood and placed her hand on the younger woman's shoulder. "Nope. It never does."

The city editor walked back to her office, leaving in her wake a new wave of speculations coursing through the newsroom. April ignored it all, as she returned to the half-finished story on her computer screen. Luckily, the routine of upcoming court dockets required very little concentration.

Slider appeared from down the doorway leading to the three darkrooms that served the paper's photographers. His face was pale as he crossed the newsroom.

"What's up, kiddo? Brian tells me your ass is grass," Slider said. April sent him a smile that returned the color to his face, but left him with an expression of confusion.

"My ass has never been this grassless before," April answered. "Sam Trimble made a special trip to my desk to compliment me on an article."

"You're kidding."

"No. I'm not."

"Jesus, was this predicted in Revelations or anything?"

April chuckled and motioned her chin across the room. "Careful, you'll have Tim Jones quoting scripture." She referred to the newspaper's religion editor. The would-be reverend had been booted out of seminary when it was discovered that he knew the dean's daughter in the Biblical sense. The poor young man still spent his life trying to make up in religious devotion what he could not seem to overcome in his taste for willing women. He'd tried most every Protestant religion available in their mid-sized city, but no easy cure had been found for his addiction. During one tearful session in the city editor's office, Kate Stevens had suggested counseling, and the would-be reverend had listened. The young women of the *Amber Daily* now found it safe to wander into the break room unescorted.

"Yeah. Hey, are you doing something you can't leave?"

April looked at the story on her computer screen. She had plenty of time to finish it before the next day's deadline.

"Nope," she answered.

"I'm souping film. Come back and keep me company for a while." Just as he spoke, the alarm on his watch beeped. "Damn." Slider bolted for the darkroom. April followed at a more leisurely pace.

"Did you make it in time?" April asked as she stood in the doorway, watching Slider pour solution into a four-roll developing tank.

"We'll know when it comes out of the fix."

Of course the *Amber Daily* photographers had long since graduated to digital photography for news stories, but, under Slider's insistence, they still maintained a darkroom. Slider firmly believed that there was an art to film photography that digital could never replace. True, he was about the only one who ever resorted to film and chemicals, but the art of his feature photos was legendary. No one dared argue with his loyalty to 35mm film. The proof was in the Associated Press awards he'd won again and again.

Slider agitated the tank briefly and then turned to face his friend. For five minutes, there was nothing for the photographer to do but wait.

April closed the door, so they could talk in peace. As the fornicating religion editor had learned, a closed darkroom door was sacred. Such knowledge had been part of what sent him to employer required counseling.

"Life's definitely going your way, kiddo," Slider said.

"No lie. Didn't know Sam liked my work all that

well."

"It's not just Sam. You really seem to have your act together right now."

"What do you mean?"

"Sure, your work is good, but you're decent company almost all the time. Heck, even your dog's happier." Slider waved his long arms expressively. "You've even got me enjoying sunsets so much I forgot to take pictures of a really good one the other night. I just watched it, like any old fool."

April paused to think. She did feel good. Getting up in the morning didn't require any noticeable effort, a fact that had not been true for much of her life.

"Yeah, I guess you're right. Must be something in the water."

It was Slider's turn to pause for thought. "How long has that discussion group…what's it called…the girl's john or something like that…how long's that been meeting?"

"The Ladies' Room," April responded, ignoring her friend's attempt to goad her. "We've been meeting for about a month."

Slider nodded slowly. "I think that's it. You've changed since you started meeting with those women."

April smiled. "I'm not surprised. Slider, I can't tell you how wonderful it feels to be able to talk about what matters to me and listen to other women who trust me."

The darkroom timer buzzed, and Slider turned his back on April as he poured fixer from the tank into its storage container.

"You know. I think I'm envious," Slider said.

April watched without seeing as he continued to work over the sink. "Slider, you should be. Maybe you could come sometime."

"I thought it was all lesbians."

"It's been all women, but not all lesbians. You know that Mo's sister, Allison, has been to every session." April laughed. "The two sorority sisters who showed up by mistake for the first meeting have even come back a time or two, but we're forbidden to tell their husbands where they've been."

"You're kidding me," Slider responded.

April's expression changed, and she struck the palm of her hand against her forehead. "Great! I just thought of something."

"What?"

"I promised weeks ago that I'd get an attorney to come speak to the group about legal issues for gay couples."

Slider finished what he was doing and turned to face April, an impish smile on his long face. "I bet I know who you ask."

April raised her chin, defiant. "Who?"

"Sophia what's her name. That lady who spoke at the Angusville city council meeting."

April was embarrassed that Slider had remembered her reaction to the woman. "Not a bad idea. She's a sharp lady."

"Yeah, right," Slider responded. "Have fun with this one, kiddo."

April didn't respond to his comment, but she secretly hoped that fun would be an added benefit to an official call to Sophia Mendez. She knew the number. Truth was, she hadn't forgotten to call. Some tasks just took a little longer. April wouldn't hesitate to call out a crooked cop or interview a murderer. But calling Sophia Mendez, now that took some real courage.

Chapter Six

April really wished she'd changed clothes. The jeans and sweater that seemed fine that morning didn't go particularly well with the leather chair on which she now rested. Even the spiral stenographer's pad she always carried looked ratty where it sat on a highly polished, cherry coffee table. Only one other person occupied the room. April smiled politely as she met the gaze of a receptionist, seated behind a desk of equal tone and quality to the solid, wooden coffee table. The receptionist returned April's smile with a slightly more mechanical version. Her gaze returned immediately to the computer screen before her. April was beginning to regret her decision to arrive early.

Funny, as a reporter, April had spent her fair share of time in lawyers' waiting rooms. This one was on the nice side, but not that much nicer. She didn't remember feeling this out of place before. As the moments ticked past, April occupied herself with her favorite pastime, self-analysis. Why in the blue blazes did she feel an adolescent awkwardness with no apparent cause? Like most reporters, she enjoyed the casual dress accepted in her profession, and didn't usually concern herself with appropriate dress code. At the start of any one day, April didn't know if she should dress for crawling around a train wreck, or a meeting with the mayor. A lack of proper dress was no excuse for failing to get the story. *Why now? Why do I care today?*

Maybe it's because I'm a client and not a reporter. That had a ring of truth to it. As a reporter, it usually mattered far more what she thought of the person being interviewed than what the individual thought of her. April's brow creased as she wondered about the unconscious arrogance she'd developed within her profession. It was not a pleasant prospect.

Alas, even self-analysis could not hold April's interest for long. She retrieved her steno pad from the table and reviewed notes from an interview with the Chamber of Commerce manager. The subject was hog farms…big hog farms…actually, only one, big, hog farm. Amber's Chamber was doing everything in its power to attract a proposed facility capable of feeding 20,000 hogs into happy oblivion. No matter how she looked at it, that was a lot of bacon to put on a lot of tables. April first checked her notes from the information the Chamber manager had given her; economic impact, number of employees. She then referred to her list of questions left unanswered; potential stress on limited water resources, background of the company slated to build the facility. In a short time, she forgot her discomfort in the plush waiting room, as her mind plotted whom to call for the missing information. Her eyes lost their focus, and her mind started forming the words for the article.

"Excuse me."

April jumped, startled back to the present. She looked up to gaze into the deepest pair of brown eyes she'd ever seen in her life.

"I'm sorry, I didn't mean to surprise you," Sophia Mendez said in a warm voice, flavored with the hint of her Mexican-American heritage. She touched April on the shoulder in a gesture of apology. April felt the brief contact like a wave of heat emanating from her shoulder. She'd forgotten the degree of attraction she'd felt for this dark-haired Latina.

"No, don't…I mean…it wasn't you. I was just a thousand miles away," April sputtered as she struggled to her feet. She looked up ever so slightly to meet the gaze of the taller woman. Sophia's smile displayed that rare inversion where the smile started with her eyes and flowed easily to her mouth.

"If you'll follow me, we can go back to my office," Sophia said.

A sign of a junior associate, the office was near the rear of the building, but April was impressed that the quality of outer office continued into Sophia's personal domain. Art by Tomás Guajardo, a framed diploma from Texas Tech law school, and a Mexican clay water jar fit perfectly with the furnishings, depicting quality professionalism. The few hints of individual personality and background told April of Sophia's deep and intense pride in her Hispanic heritage. April was pleased. She knew a few minority professionals who had become white in all but skin color.

"Please, sit down," Sophia motioned to a chair in front of her desk. April was slightly disconcerted as the attorney took a chair opposite April's rather than the one behind the desk. Sophia picked up a leather-bound notebook and a gold pen.

"So, how may I help you?" Sophia asked.

"I hope you don't feel that I'm abusing my free consultation when I tell you that I'm here to ask a favor rather than retain you as an attorney."

"Yes?" Sophia raised one eyebrow, and April wondered how many requests this attractive, obviously compassionate woman received for free assistance. April fought with a twinge of guilt and determined that she would take as little of the attorney's time as possible.

"I'm facilitating a…a women's discussion group, and we've had some legal issues arise. We are looking for an attorney to present a program addressing some of those issues."

"And what are those issues?"

April's mouth went dry. It was not a new sensation. Even after many years, she always felt that wave of fear the first time she came out to a new person.

"Domestic partnership and legal complications relating to that."

"Do you mean matters such as the provisions for common law marriage once a man and a woman reside together for a specified period?"

"No." April could feel her sweaty fingers adhering to the cardboard cover on her steno pad. She raised her chin proudly as she decided on the direct approach. "This is a lesbian discussion group."

Mild surprise registered on Sophia's face before her gaze made a journey from April's worn, leather lace-ups and finally stopped at April's makeup-less eyes. The attorney's dignified manner never wavered, but there was a brief "I should have realized" look on her face.

"I hope you're not offended at the prospect of meeting with a group of gay women," April said, a hint of challenge in her voice.

"Not at all," Sophia said with a soft smile.

Whatever surprise she may have felt was now enveloped in composure. She bent her head and scribbled a note. "I can certainly see that lesbians would have some legal complications in maintaining a domestic partnership. Are there any couples with children?"

"Not in our group…not yet," April paused to laugh. "Actually, there are, but they're straight women with husbands."

"I thought you said this was a lesbian discussion group."

"We're not prejudiced. One of our regular members is a straight woman who comes with her sister, who's a lesbian." April laughed. "There are two other married mothers who come occasionally."

"Why do you find that amusing?"

"They misunderstood a notice in the newspaper for our first meeting and thought they were going to a sorority meeting to discuss families."

Sophia's laugh temporarily evaporated her composure, and April caught a glimpse of how the woman enjoyed life. "I'm sure that was interesting." She tilted her head, confused. "But they came back?"

"Yeah, I've been confused about that, too. One of them said that being around women who didn't have to worry about pleasing a man gave her a whole new perspective on life." April glanced at the gold wedding ring Sophia wore. She had noticed it, with great disappointment, just after they arrived in the office. "Maybe you'll find the same is true for you."

Sophia blushed, and April hated herself for causing the wave of pain that passed through her warm, dark eyes. "I fear it is too late," Sophia said. "I am divorced."

April sighed as she looked at her shoes. "I'll say

I'm sorry, but I know it won't help. Wish I could take my question back."

"Didn't you say you were a reporter?"

"Yes."

"I thought reporters never regretted a question."

"Part of being a good reporter is knowing when something's none of your business."

The eyebrow rose again. "I'll try to remember that the next time I'm answering a reporter's questions."

April laughed. "If this were business, I wouldn't be as concerned for your feelings."

Sophia smiled. "I see."

"So, are you interested in speaking to our group?"

"What are the specific issues?"

April's face turned serious. "One of our ladies is about to have major surgery. She wants to know how to make sure that her lover, and not her family, will be calling the shots if any decisions need to be made while she's under the anesthetic. She's also concerned that, if anything happens during surgery, her family doesn't take away half of what she and Sandy have built together."

"I can bring standard forms for living wills and limited powers of attorney for the medical decisions, but I advise them to see an attorney about a will," Sophia said.

"They'd hear that a lot better if it came from you."

"I must say, I find that thought intriguing." Sophia laughed.

"What's funny?"

"When this firm hired me, they told me frankly that they hoped I could attract minority clients."

April smiled. "But you don't think we're the

minority they want?"

Sophia laughed. "They won't object, but they may be surprised."

The two women compared calendars and set Sophia's visit to the Ladies' Room. April realized with regret that there was no longer any reason for her to loiter in Sophia Mendez' office.

"I guess I should ask if you need a speaker's fee or something. I'll warn you that the group isn't exactly rolling in bucks."

"The firm encourages us to contribute a certain amount of time to public service. I'd say that this applies."

"Great." Reluctantly, April stood. "I can't tell you how much we appreciate your help."

Sophia extended her hand, and April took it gratefully as they exchanged a business-like handshake. "I'm sure I'll enjoy the experience," Sophia answered.

April left the office hoping beyond hope that Sophia would do just that.

❧❧❧❧

A thirty-pound fur ball launched itself ecstatically at April, as she opened the front door to her home.

"Take it easy, Nearly. I know I'm late. I had business," April told the bouncing blonde ball that she knew would turn into her faithful dog once the excitement passed. April crossed quickly to the back door and let her dog out to the doggie bathroom. Nearly completed her business in short order and was scratching at the door before April had her coat hung in the closet.

When Nearly was a puppy, April had assumed that the greeting ritual would eventually become less enthusiastic. Nearly was now five years old, and April had learned to live with her enthusiastic housemate. Her day was not complete if the dog did not bound directly from the ground to stick her nose in her mistress's face at least once. At least, after much yelling and aversion training, it was just a nose and not a long, wet tongue expressing the dog's joy.

April plopped on the couch, and the dog calmed, resting her head on the woman's knee. It was now time for the "Do you want to hear about my day?" ritual. The dog's intent expression as she listened had been the main motivator for her name, Nearly Human.

"I had a really great day, Nearly." April looked around in a mock search for listeners who were not there. "I'll tell you a secret." She leaned down to whisper into a canine ear. "I met with a very special woman today." It was still a hope that she would dare admit only to her dog.

Chapter Seven

An unusually large number of dishes covered the buffet table, a sure sign of a successful meeting of the Ladies' Room Discussion Group. An even surer sign was the near emptiness of each of those dishes. A well fed group was a happy group. April glanced at the table, smiling as she thought of it as a typical example of the lesbian potluck.

"Any unmarried couple, whether heterosexual or homosexual, must take an active interest in their legal status if they wish to protect their partner," Sophia Mendez stated. April's attention returned to the attorney. She joined the roomful of women who now directed their full attention to the dark-eyed beauty expressing an excellent understanding of the law.

"You mean, like this limited power of attorney?" Sandy asked, waving a form Sophia had provided for all the women.

"Yes," Sophia added. "If a person is unconscious and medical decisions must be made, the law makes certain assumptions about who has a right to make those decisions. If you fail to prepare a limited power of attorney for your…partners, then the law assumes that your nearest blood relative has a right to make decisions concerning your health and well-being."

Tandy shuddered visibly. "That's not a pleasant thought. Not a pleasant thought at all." She was paying the weekend bartender overtime so that she and Sharon could attend the presentation.

Sophia glanced at her notes, and waved the small stack of legal forms she had duplicated for distribution to the entire group. "These documents are very rudimentary." Her smile lightened the room, and as April looked at the faces before her, she knew she was not alone in fantasies about this straight visitor. "At the risk of sounding like I'm drumming up business, I'd really recommend that the couples in this room seriously visit with an attorney to prepare customized wills and to determine if other legal agreements are needed to protect your partners."

Sandy leaned forward, grinning at the visiting attorney. "Honey, you can expect a phone call from us in the morning."

"Us too," Tandy added.

Sophia laughed. "I'll look forward to it." The Latina continued in her letter-perfect English with just a hint of an accent. "That's all that I have for tonight. I truly enjoyed meeting you all." A murmur of gratitude rippled through the room.

April glanced at her watch. "Good grief, women. We've grilled this poor lady for nearly two hours." She smiled at Sophia, trying to control the expression of personal admiration her heart felt for the attorney. "We thank you very much for visiting our group."

"Took some guts to come here," one woman said. It was her first night at the Ladies' Room, and April made a mental note to get her name and address before she left.

Billboard jumped up from the informal seat she had taken on the floor. "Great program, Ms. Mendez. So, who wants a beer?"

A ripple of laughter broke the serious mood that surrounded Sophia's lessons on legal pitfalls. Some of the women, especially those in committed relationships, still felt a cold fear at the thought of legal vulnerability to families or even ex-husbands. Several hands held the stack of legal forms in death grips, assuring that they would not be lost before they arrived safely at home. The babble of voices and flurry of activity was soon in full flow as women retrieved dishes from the buffet table, or waved and called their goodbyes as Billboard led a contingent down to the Pink Triangle.

April stayed at Sophia's side, playing the role of protector. She congratulated herself on the wisdom of presenting the attorney with a "Straight, but not Narrow" button when Sophia first arrived. Despite the message pinned openly on the shoulder of her suit jacket, the litigator turned down at least three invitations for a drink, before the crowd thinned and then faded. Finally, a quiet hush replaced the babble as Tandy and Sharon remained to help April with the final check and clean up. April didn't know why Sophia stayed behind, but she was glad of a few more minutes of the Latina's company.

"You sure did a dandy job tonight," Tandy said, as she folded the legs of a card-table.

"Thank you," Sophia answered. "I'm not just being polite when I tell you that I enjoyed the evening. It's so refreshing to be in a room full of women who are…" her brows creased as she searched for the right word, "…unafraid."

April laughed with little humor. "Don't let us fool you. We're plenty scared."

"Amen to that," Sharon added.

Sophia sat, obviously unready to depart. "Perhaps that is not exactly what I meant to say." She shook her head, trying to form her impression into words. "I don't really mean that I saw a lack of fear. Perhaps a better description would be that this was a room filled with women of courage."

Tandy stopped as she placed cups in the trash. "What do you mean?"

Sophia smiled softly. For an instant, April felt in the attorney the trust that, one by one, she had seen on the faces of all the women of the Ladies' Room. "When I answered Stella's question about her family's right to make medical decisions for her under certain circumstances, Sandy looked as if she could fight the world and win."

April laughed. "Sometimes I think Sandy could do just that."

"There was a little of that in all your faces," Sophia answered. "When I am among…should I say normal women?"

"We prefer straight," Tandy answered.

"When I am around straight women, they do not realize that they can fight the rest of the world. They…I…was taught that a woman must adapt to her world, be compliant with the men in her life. I don't think most women feel like society gives them permission to have courage."

Sharon sat beside her. "I've got a friend, a straight man, who said something interesting to me one day. He said that when he was a kid, his parents tried to teach him what was right, but, one day, he realized that among the good, they'd filled his head with a lot of shit. It just takes a little while to shake out the shit."

"You didn't finish law school and make a life for

yourself without a pretty good dose of courage," April commented.

Sophia looked up, and April's heart constricted as she saw the glisten of tears in those dark eyes. "Yes, but until tonight, I did not feel I had a right to that courage."

"Hot dog," Tandy exclaimed.

"What?" Sharon asked.

"Finally, now I understand why those straight sorority women keep coming back to the Ladies' Room." They all laughed. "I heard you turn down some invitations for a drink, but I'll invite you anyway. It'd be on the house. That's the least we can do for all your free advice."

"Thank you, Tandy, but I wouldn't...I wouldn't feel comfortable," Sophia answered.

"I'm sorry Sophia, but you look like you need to talk about what you learned here tonight, and Sharon and I have to go back down to the bar. I'm playing hooky, you know."

"Certainly, I understand," Sophia answered, standing as she realized the conversation must end.

April took a deep breath, gathering her courage. "I'm available. How about I buy you some pie and coffee as a small payment for your kindness."

"What kind of pie?"

"Any kind they've got in the cooler at the Blackstone Cafe?"

"*Muy bien*," Sophia answered.

"I don't think they'll have any of that, but they make a great coconut cream," April answered.

Tandy threw a magazine at her friend. "Don't let her fool you, Sophia. She speaks Spanish just fine."

"I know, I've heard."

"Heard where?" April asked.

"Yes, from the people living in the San Juan *colonia* in Angusville."

April felt her heart lurch. She didn't realize Sophia had even known she was there. It was a very pleasant realization.

❧ ❧ ❧ ❧

The Blackstone was the Blackstone, was the Blackstone. By any other name it would still look like a 1940s hole in the wall, but April loved it. At least it was clean…if you didn't look too close. She'd discovered the cafe her first week working for the *Amber Daily*, and she'd only grown to love it more with time. April maintained an unexplainable fascination with anachronisms. Sometimes, when she ate lunch alone at the worn Formica and chrome counter, she looked through half-closed eyes at the cook plopping steaming plates in the service window, and, for just a moment, seventy years disappeared. She could feel the energy of the young men at the DeSoto Hotel, across the street, as they waited anxiously for the bus taking them to boot camp, the first leg on their journey to war in the unknown lands of Europe and the Pacific.

Tonight, she cared too much about the here and now to think of a war long ended. The company of the woman sitting in the booth across from her provided as much adventure as she wanted…at least for now. As she looked at the graceful movements of Sophia's slender hands and glanced at the fine cut of the attorney's gray suit, April felt a sudden anxiety about her choice of a restaurant.

"I probably should have given you some options

about where to go for dessert," April offered.

"Why? I've had their pie, and it's excellent."

April looked around her favorite cafe. "I guess it is a little shabby in here."

Sophia laughed. "What did you say on the drive here...that it had character?"

"That it does. Hope you don't mind this particular kind of character."

The attorney looked around the room. "Not at all. Besides, eating in traditional cafes like this makes me feel a little thrill of victory."

"What do you mean?"

Momentarily, Sophia's eyes reflected a passion that surprised April. Then the Latina dropped her gaze and the electric sense of connection was broken.

"Did you realize that when the Blackstone Cafe first opened, people of color, any color but white that is, were not allowed to eat here?"

April felt the realization like a punch to the stomach. "I...I'm sorry."

"Why? You didn't do it."

The reporter shrugged. "Guess I can't help but feel a little corporate guilt."

Sophia leaned across the table and placed her hand on April's arm, passion once again reflected in her eyes. "Don't you realize how wonderful it was to have you take me here without even pausing to wonder about my being Hispanic?

"I don't understand." April mourned the loss of warmth, as Sophia took her hand from April's arm.

"I meant what I said. It feels like a victory eating in a...," Sophia paused, looking for an apt description.

"Redneck cafe."

The Latina laughed. "Excellent description.

Anyway, my right to eat pie and coffee at the Blackstone reminds me that we are making a better world."

"*Poco a poco*," April observed.

"*Sí*, little by little," Sophia responded

The waitress sidled up to the table in typical 1940s style. She wore a faded, blue uniform, complete with the starched and useless cap that required at least four bobby pins just to stay on her head. April was surprised at her resentment of the waitress's intrusion on their space. The two women each ordered coconut cream pie, a legend among Blackstone aficionadas, and were left alone once again.

"April, I'm very glad you remembered my name from the city council meeting."

"So am I." April squirmed in her seat as she balanced her need for good sense with an awareness that she would always regret any lost opportunity with this woman. "I hope you aren't too uncomfortable with this coming from a lesbian, but, Sophia Mendez, you are not an easy woman to forget."

Sophia turned her face to the side and dropped her gaze. April could see the other woman's heightened color as she blushed.

"Now I've embarrassed you. I'm sorry," April said.

"No, not at all." Sophia struggled to regain her composure. "I just don't know what to say...or even feel. I've never had to think about..."

"How to respond when another woman tells you you're beautiful," April said. She took a quick swallow of ice water, trying to overcome the sudden dryness in her throat.

Sophia looked directly into April's eyes. "Yes. This is not a situation my mother thought to prepare me for."

"Come on. Didn't she ever tell you to watch out for 'that type of woman?'"

Sophia laughed. "If it weren't for television, I'm not sure I ever would have known there were 'that type of women.' I didn't hear the word lesbian until I was in high school when some of my classmates were gossiping about the basketball team. At first, I thought it meant a woman who was good at sports."

"Hey, maybe you were right." April laughed. "Guess your mother was a little shy on giving the facts of life."

"A little! *Madre de Dios*! If it hadn't been for health class and the family dog, I would have gone to my wedding night completely mystified."

The subject was taking an uncomfortable turn, "How'd that go?"

"Better than the marriage," Sophia mumbled.

The waitress interrupted as she placed pie and coffee before the women. April picked up her fork, but barely noticed the fluffy concoction before her.

"I'm sorry," she said. "I didn't mean to open old wounds."

A sad smile played at Sophia's lips. "I'm glad you did. I feel very comfortable talking with you."

April's face flushed with pleasure. "I'm glad."

Sophia cut daintily at her pie. Her eyes opened in pleased surprise, as she took the first bite. "This really is good."

"Redneck cafes do get some things right."

"My family is very traditional and very Catholic. Once I was married, they considered me my husband's property. When I refused to quit college, there were problems between my husband and me, and it got worse with time.”

“No kids?”

Sophia released a shaky sigh. “No, and I never had the courage to tell my mother that I made sure there would be no children, at least not until I was ready.”

“Whoops! A Catholic using birth control…and you said you admired our courage. Sounds like you’re a woman who knows what you want.”

Sophia placed her fork forcibly on the table. “I knew I would never accept the life of slavery I’d seen in my mother and my aunts.”

April halted mid-chew. She didn’t want to interrupt even with the sound of her eating.

There were tears, old and hidden, teasing at Sophia’s eyes. “Perhaps I never should have married, but I could not deny everything my family expected, and I did care for Rudolfo until…”

April knew the rest of the sentence. She had seen it too many times before. After three years of service on the Amber Rape Crisis/Domestic Violence Board of Directors, she’d learned more than she ever wanted to know. “Until he started beating you.”

“Yes,” Sophia responded, her voice barely a whisper. She had lost all interest in her pie. “And he… he…”

“Raped you when you didn’t give him what he wanted,” April finished. She placed her hands under the table, trying to hide how they shook with fury.

“Yes,” Sophia answered so quietly that April saw, more than heard, the word leave her lips.

“Have you ever talked about it?”

“Some. When I was in law school, I finally told an instructor I trusted. She insisted I see a counselor. I thought…I thought I'd put it all behind me."

April stirred her coffee that needed no stirring. "Bad things happen, Sophia. Sometimes I think it's a mistake to put them behind us. They never leave you. I guess the choice isn't to forget or remember, but whether to use them to find courage or to admit defeat." She smiled sadly. "If you haven't noticed lady, you've chosen to find courage."

Sophia's face lit with a joy made richer by the pain. "Thank you, April. I cannot tell you how much it means to hear that."

"Thank you for trusting me enough to have a chance to say it."

The Latina shook her head. "And why do I trust you? I barely know you."

"Hey, I'm a reporter, remember? Don't forget. Always trust your instincts."

"Yes," Sophia responded, her voice barely a whisper.

Chapter Eight

Slider pulled his dinged and dented Chevy, into a parking space in front of the Northeast Amber Holiness Church. The photographer was not happy. He didn't mind working evenings or nights when the scanner rousted him out to a fire, wreck, or potential riot, a news photographer's dream. Those were just parts of his job. Darned if he'd ever ask another favor of Hank Thomas, the official advertising photog. Hank had reviewed, edited, and selected Tri-State Fair photos when Slider was still out shooting the fair and couldn't meet the day's deadline without help. The veteran photographer had known what would happen, even as he delegated the task to the advertising photog, but he didn't have much choice. Hank was a legend at the payback he demanded for any favor. It could come at any time in any form. April once asked Hank to shoot a public building dedication because the news photogs were all busy. A month later, April found herself the unwilling dog sitter of Hank's unfriendly shar-pei. The wrinkled mutt and Nearly mixed like oil and water. April spent the entire two weeks of Hank's vacation with her house physically divided into war zones. Slider had helped build the plywood barriers that kept the two dogs from killing each other.

Could be worse, Slider thought, as he looked at the brown brick of the squarish, simple church building. It should be a quick shoot, even if he had to interrupt a quiet Wednesday evening at home. After all, the church was paying good money for a quarter-page add about their upcoming revival. If they wanted a shot of their church with the congregation inside, they'd have it. Slider was just grateful they'd allowed him to visit the Wednesday evening service instead of attending Sunday morning.

The strap of the camera bag fit comfortably in its familiar groove over Slider's right shoulder. He already had the Nikon loaded with fresh batteries, and he planned on getting in and out as soon as possible. He could hear the sound of a traditional hymn, one that made Slider think of his grandmother, as an enthusiastic pianist accompanied an equally enthusiastic congregation. Slider wore his usual jeans, but he'd substituted an Oxford shirt for the usual t-shirt, and he wore one of his three ties, the one without cartoon characters. Slider took a deep breath and walked inside the church. He found a seat at the back and removed the camera from the bag. The congregation continued the song until the final notes died in a barrage of flourishes from the piano. Although the sanctuary was not full, Slider thought he could achieve the desired effect by carefully choosing the angle of his shot. Reverend Thomas asked for pictures of an attentive audience listening reverently to the words of God. On the drive over, Slider had translated the instructions into "the old fart wants everyone to see how important he is to his people." Even without her presence, the photographer could hear April's warning to keep his opinions to himself while he was in enemy territory. It wasn't that Slider didn't like churches. He didn't like much of anything that made him feel he needed to conform.

"Well, brothers and sisters," an overweight minister sporting a flat-top haircut said, as he stepped to the podium. Slider recognized the voice of Reverend Thomas from their telephone conversation. "We have a special blessing tonight. A photographer from the *Amber Daily* is here to take pictures for the ad on our upcoming revival. Now all of you need to encourage the poor lost souls who may see this advertisement. I want you all sitting at the sides and toward the back to gather toward the front."

The minister encouraged his congregation with a warm smile and a welcoming wave of his hand. Slider was surprised at how quickly the congregation complied. The movement vaguely reminded him of sheep neatly herded into a pen. Slider went to work, snapping photos as the minister spoke, and shoved his mental commentary to the back of his thoughts. He concentrated not so much on Reverend Thomas's words or his own reactions, as to the visual effect he sought to achieve. It was easy. For the most part, the people did listen attentively, especially the women. Slider was surprised by their uniformity, all dressed in calf-length cotton dresses, and long hair neatly wrapped and pinned in only slightly differing versions of a French bun. He moved, seeking angles less likely to emphasize the sameness of those women. The reverend droned on, without Slider bothering to listen …until the message took a drastic turn…one that sent a shiver of fear into Slider's heart. His halfhearted listening detected the essence of the message, a tirade on the hazards of evil. One word focused Slider's full attention on the minister's words. The minister's voice dripped rage and contempt as he spoke a simple noun

...as he spoke of "homosexuals."

"My friends, my beloved flock," Reverend Thomas said, a quaver of practiced sincerity in his voice. "I must speak to you again of the abomination that threatens the very core of our society." Slider lowered the camera, looking with his unfiltered vision at the reddened and angry face of the minister. "Our community continues to fail to heed my warnings of the decadent growth of this malignancy called homosexuality in our city."

A deep amen erupted from a man sitting near the front, and Slider felt his mouth grow dry.

"These people...these creatures, who dare call their lifestyle gay as though it could bring any form of happiness...defy the very natural ways decreed by our Creator," Thomas bellowed so passionately that he sent a thin spray of saliva over the podium and toward the altar. "I shall continue to write my letters. I shall continue to voice my warnings, but remember this...you of my flock sent here by God to receive my guidance..." His voice went soft and threatening, and Slider felt the presence of the man's hate like a living, breathing creature. "In the end, these homosexuals must be stopped...whatever the costs."

Slider stuffed his camera back in the bag, not caring if he had all the shots he needed. He was out the church and in the car before the minister completed another sentence. It only took a few minutes for Slider to reach April's house. She needed to hear about this.

❧❧❧❧

April enjoyed the warmth of the sun against the side of her face as she drove. Her skin felt dry and papery from a day spent in the wind, and not even liberal applications of sunscreen prevented the slight burn she'd received. Not the sunburn, not even Slider's dire warnings voiced the night before could detract from April's pleasure in the day. She and Sophia drove in silence, both mildly tired from their long hike in the canyon. Even without conversation, April enjoyed the growing sense of companionship.

All too soon, they arrived at Sophia's house. April pulled her car into the driveway and smiled shyly at her companion.

"I still can't believe you'd never made the hike to Saddle Rock before," April said.

"Never."

"And you grew up around here?"

"What can I say? With six children, my parents didn't have the energy to organize long hikes, and I've been far too busy with my studies and then my career," Sophia answered.

April grinned. "You need to learn how to play."

As though on cue, Nearly Human popped up from his nap in the backseat, slung a filthy paw over Sophia's shoulder and lovingly licked the dark-haired woman on the ear. Sophia leveled a less than loving look at the dog.

"Your dog agrees."

"And some folks just train their dogs to sit."

Sophia laughed a deep, throaty chuckle. The sound made April short of breath, and she turned her full attention to the keys hanging from the ignition as she turned off the engine. She feared the Latina would see the blush beneath her sunburn.

"Will you come in for a while?" Sophia asked. "I've a fresh pitcher of prickly pear tea in the refrigerator."

April licked dry lips. "Cold liquid sounds tempting, the tepid water in my canteen wasn't hacking it for the last mile or two, but what would I do with the mongrel here?"

Sophia reached to scratch Nearly behind the ears, finding just the right spot to make the dog moan with pleasure. "I'll wager our four-legged friend wouldn't mind a bowl of cool water. My back yard is fenced. He can wait there."

"Sold!" April threw open her door and whistled for Nearly to follow.

The confusion as they herded the dog around the house and through the back gate helped April hide the apprehension she felt at entering Sophia's house. Since their first meeting, April spent at least a few minutes every night, reminding herself that the beautiful Hispanic woman was as straight as a pin. Despite all her internal warnings, those last few moments before sleep lulled her mind into the hidden world of dreamland were spent remembering Sophia's mellow voice, the sparkle of her dark eyes, and the graceful movements of strong but delicate hands. Put simply, April had it bad.

Still, April was no youth, blinded by love. She knew enough of life to realize that some of the best friendships grew out of one-sided loves. Perhaps, if she'd been wise, April would have protected her heart by avoiding the company of this beautiful woman. That wasn't April's philosophy. If Sophia was worth loving, she was certainly worth having as a friend.

April took the cool glass of tea Sophia offered and downed its contents in two swallows.

"Hey, that stuff's good," April said.

"How would you know? You didn't take time to taste it."

April grinned as she pulled off her ball cap and used her forearm to brush back hair still sweaty from the long hike. "I'll do better next time. Can I have more?"

Sophia laughed the laugh that haunted April as she slept, letting loose in her dreams the longing she could not freely express. "I suppose." The Latina sipped at her tea with more composure than her companion. "I could use a refill as well."

While Sophia retreated to the kitchen, April studied the room around her. She enjoyed this alone time to view Sophia's personal space. It helped satisfy her hunger to learn more. The living room was neat and clean, filled with quality furniture chosen more for comfort than pretentiousness. The overall style displayed an easy combination of Sophia's Hispanic heritage and the modern taste of an independent, professional woman. An R. C. Gorman print gave evidence to an interest in Native American studies, and the handcarved Our Lady of Guadalupe positioned over the center of the mantel testified to continued ties to Sophia's Catholic roots. Sufficient clutter, mainly magazines and newspapers, covered the coffee table to prove that Sophia believed her home was a place to live and not keep as a show piece. April moved to the bookcase, checking the titles for clues as to Sophia's heart and mind. She barely had time to note that Spanish titles filled the shelf, when Sophia returned, an ice-filled glass in each hand.

"Please, sit down. You don't have to wander around my home like a lost puppy," Sophia said, as she kicked off her shoes and curled into a corner of the couch.

April briefly eyed an overstuffed chair before deciding to indulge her masochistic need to be near the attorney and took a seat at the opposite end of the couch. A comfortable distance still separated them, but the knowledge that no real obstacles separated her from her heart's desire gave April a secret thrill. April sighed as she relaxed into the comfort of the cushions after the exertion of their hike. April concentrated on sipping more slowly at her second glass of tea.

"This really is good tea," she said.

"My grandmother used to make her own, drying bits of prickly pear buttons to mix with the tea. Now, I just buy it every time I go to Santa Fe."

"Would your grandmother approve?"

Sophia laughed. "She'd have me buy it by the case. It saved her having to pick and dry the cactus buttons." Sadness deepened the brown of Sophia's eyes. "Those last few years, the arthritis in her hands made it difficult for her to do many things she had done all her life."

April spotted a coaster and set her tea on the table. She felt the need to free her hands, fighting the urge to offer comfort for the loss expressed on Sophia's face.

"When did she die?" April asked.

Sophia closed her eyes as she remembered. "Nearly six years ago."

"You miss her?"

"Badly. She was always a touch of sanity no matter what happened in my life."

"Was it your grandparents who immigrated from Mexico?"

Sophia laughed and there was a sparkle in her

eye as she smiled at April. "Even you, *mija*. Don't tell me you think like all the *gringos*."

April blushed. "Whoops! What did I say?"

"My family came from New Mexico near Espanola. My people lived in this area before you Anglos even dreamed to dare the Santa Fe Trail."

"But you grew up in Angusville. I thought all the Hispanic families there immigrated from Mexico when the truck farms started during World War II."

"Most did. My father was a young man and there wasn't much work in Espanola. He and my mother came to work the onion fields."

A slow smile crossed April's face. "I bet you get a real bang out of it when the rednecks try to tell you to go back where you came from."

"If those of us living on the Llano Estacado needed residential seniority to stay, I could send all you Anglos packing."

April molded her face into a contrite expression. "Can I stay?"

Sophia leaned across the couch and touched April's cheek. "Of course, *mija*. I'd say you're worth keeping."

The Latina's gentle touch was over in an instant, but April felt a pleasant heat start at her cheek and make its way rapidly to her heart. She took a deep, shaky breath.

"Don't do that," she said.

"Do what?" Sophia asked.

April looked at the other woman with an intensity she wished was not there. "Touch me."

Sophia leaned back. Her eyes moved rapidly as her mind processed through all that April told her with those two words. April retrieved her tea and stared into the glass as though all answers for humanity could be found in the melting ice. The silence continued.

"Sorry," April finally mumbled. "I promise to be a lady." She turned a mildly defiant look toward her companion. "But you shouldn't play with the heart of your friendly neighborhood lesbo." She took a deep breath and placed her glass back on the table. "Guess I'd better go." She felt her face flush in embarrassment as she leaned forward.

"Please, don't." The pleading note in Sophia's voice made April turn to her in surprise. The Latina reached to grasp her companion's arm and then pulled back just short of touching, obviously uncertain as to what to do. April was surprised at Sophia's temporary lack of composure.

April rested against the back of the couch, carefully keeping her distance from the other woman. "I guess we need to talk about this, don't we?"

Sophia sighed and waved her hands before her, uncharacteristically at a loss for words. "April, how… how did you know you were…gay?"

April laughed. "Fairly simple really. I realized pretty young that I liked girls."

"What do you mean, 'liked girls?'" Sophia asked.

"Jeez, Sophia. Do you really want me to get into this?"

Sophia met April's gaze directly. She licked dry lips, and April was surprised at the fear she saw in the other woman's eyes.

"Yes, April. I would like to know."

"You're scared, aren't you?" April asked.

"Yes."

"Sophia, surely you know I'd never…"

"I trust you as much as I've ever trusted anyone,"

Sophia answered. "You're an honorable woman."

"Then why are you afraid?"

"Please, just answer my question."

April looked deeply into Sophia's gaze. She felt the intensity of the moment, knowing instinctively that they now shared a critical connection...a life changing instant. April took a deep breath, relying on instinct as she proceeded.

"I dated boys some when I was in school...it was expected, but it was my best friend I dreamed of at night. I knew I felt a thrill when she touched me, but ...hell, I didn't even know the word homosexual then. I didn't know what I was feeling. I just knew how I felt. It wasn't until I went into the Navy, right after high school, that I really discovered what it was all about. I got very close to Joy, one of my classmates in boot camp. She was a little more knowledgeable than me." April blushed. "I proved to be a quick study."

"How...did you..." Sophia sighed, gathering courage. "Did you ever experience a man?"

April's blush deepened. "Yeah. I dated a guy in high school for a couple of years. Raging hormones are raging hormones, and he was a decent sort. I cared about him as best I could, I guess."

"Did you hate it?"

April stared at her fingers, feeling it was important that she know exactly what she was answering. "You mean sex with a man?"

"Yes."

"No. It was okay, especially after we got over the initial awkwardness. But it was just okay. I knew the first time Joy kissed me what it was I really wanted."

They sat in silence. April gave Sophia a few moments to process.

"Okay, your turn," April said.

Sophia looked up, frightened. "What do you mean?"

"You're not just being nosy. You're asking these questions for a reason."

Sophia's fingers played across the top of her glass. She took a deep breath. "I have wondered..."

The incomplete sentence hung in the air like an overpowering weight. "About yourself?" April asked, terrified and excited at the possibilities.

"Yes," Sophia finally whispered. She leaned the back of her head against the couch and closed her eyes. April watched Sophia's face as the emotional floodgate opened. A tear trickled from the edge of her eye and down one cheek. "I married because it was expected. It was such a relief when I was finally free. Since then I have felt so...cold. Plenty of men ask for my time and attention. They think I ignore them because I am so dedicated to my work." There was a deep pain in Sophia's eyes as she looked into April's face. "I ignore them because I can feel no...fire. I have always known more passion in the courtroom than the bedroom. I had thought I would never feel as others say they do until..." Sophia looked into April's eyes and the words froze on her tongue. April was amazed to see the courageous attorney obviously paralyzed by fear.

Sophia looked lost, unsure of how to proceed. April was not. She was terrified, but not lost. She knew exactly what to do.

As their lips touched, electricity vibrated down both their bodies and poured out into the room like a visible aura. April held back, using only her lips in the uninvited kiss, afraid of offering more than Sophia could accept. It was Sophia who grasped the front of

April's shirt, pulling her close until they were in each other's arms. The kiss deepened and continued. April could feel Sophia's rapid heartbeat match her own, and she heard the Latina's soft moan as April's mouth quested to find the soft skin of Sophia's neck and shoulder.

"You're right about that first kiss," Sophia whispered breathlessly against April's ear.

Sophia's hands felt warm against April's back as the lawyer's delicate fingers traced an unformed pattern. April wrapped her arms tightly against the other woman, wanting still more…to touch more, feel more, do more. With all the strength of will within her, April pulled away, placing a hand on each of Sophia's shoulders.

"Why do you stop?" Sophia asked, the brown of her eyes deep with passion.

"I care for you, Sophia. I…I think I could love you," April answered.

"Is that bad?"

"I have to know that I'm more than an experiment for you."

Sophia touched her face. "In a moment you have made me feel the fire."

"Right now I'm confused…and I think you are too," April said. "Aren't you?"

The Latina looked away. "I feel much that I don't yet understand."

April kissed her again, with passion, but restraint, as though she installed a governor on the accelerator of her passion. "I need to think and so do you," April said.

She stood abruptly. Sophia moved in synchrony, her body obviously unwilling to break the contact.

The attorney closed her eyes and inhaled deeply. "I know that you are right." She moved her hand under April's arm and caressed the small of the other woman's back. "But I do not want you to go."

The threat of tears added highlights to the sparkle in April's eyes.

"I want us to start right," April said. "It's important to me."

Sophia laid her head on April's shoulder, and April encircled her in her arms. "*Madre de Dios*, you give me an answer I have wanted for many years and now you wish to turn away."

"No, dear," April said, as she used a forefinger to raise Sophia's face so that you she could look into the other woman's eyes. "You need time to think…to know that this is really what you want. I want you to know how much I respect and appreciate you." April's eyes took on the distant stare of memory. "There were times I hated Joy because I didn't fully understand what I had begun. I don't want that for you. In time, I figured it all out and knew that she gave me a great gift, but I don't want that kind of beginning for you."

Sophia leaned back. "All right. I…I think I understand."

April kissed her again.

"When will I see you again?" Sophia asked, breathless.

"You'd better do some serious thinking overnight, because if I have to go much longer without seeing you, I think I'll go out of my mind."

Sophia laughed, a deep throaty laugh. "*Mañana, querida*."

"*Mañana*," April answered.

Chapter Nine

Mañana got delayed. A phone call from Sam Trimble, the city editor, brought April out of a sound sleep just as daylight mixed with the darkness of night. The editor assigned April the task of covering a massive train derailment near a little town in the southeast corner of the *Amber News's* service area. Mo hadn't been happy at April's call asking if she could leave Nearly with Mo's pack of three mutts. April barely took time to drop off the dog before she headed for the boondocks. Slider was already on his way. By the time April arrived, he'd shot two rolls and a slew more on digital. He was ready to head back to the newsroom. If he hurried, there'd be art for the evening paper. April's job wasn't so easy. The year before, she'd written an expose about the condition of railroad tracks in the sparsely populated country between Amber and San Angelo. Sam wanted a follow-up, and that meant tough questions to sullen railroad employees and hours spent hunting down and checking official accident records. Late that evening, from the tiny and drafty room in Twist Junction's only motel, April heard the line click as the motel clerk listened. Awareness of the unwanted listener made the call strained and breathless, and accomplished little except to let Sophia know that April hadn't dropped off the face of the earth. Although the phone tapping was most likely spying for railroad interests, it put a damper on any personal conversation. Cell signal was non-existent in the remote area, and April felt intense frustration at the inability to express what she felt. The next day wasn't much better. April finally arrived back at the office in the early afternoon. She barely had time to write a follow-up to the abbreviated story she'd phoned in the day before. Sam Trimble wanted the full blow-by-blow. He ordered sandwiches and coffee, and kept April in his office long after the paper went to bed, wanting to learn every nuance she'd discovered, hoping with the passion of an old-fashioned newspaper man that they'd found a story with real meat to it. April barely managed an escape in time to leave for the Ladies' Room discussion group.

"My, oh, my, don't you look wild-eyed?" Johnnie said, as she paused in arranging food on the snack table.

"Thanks," April grumbled. "It's been a tough couple of days."

"I told everyone you were gone," Mo said. "Your dog's still in my backyard."

"Sorry, Mo. I haven't had time to go pick him up. I just left the office."

Allison looked at her watch. "Little late isn't it?"

"Yeah, Sam wanted to know all about..." April shook her head, feeling a headache return. "Sorry guys, I'm too tired to talk about it."

Johnnie stepped behind April and kneaded the knotted muscles in her neck. "You just sit down and rest, honey. Your friends will take care of you."

April obeyed Johnnie and dropped to a seat on the couch. She felt the tension ease, as she listened to the small groups of two and three chat in a babble of conversation. Most of the original Ladies' Room crew was there, including one of the straight sorority women. Their first visit may have been a mistake, but they came back out of a fascination with the lesbian perspective. Even the straight visitors were now part of a familiar and safe place. April felt the secure surroundings of family. As she relaxed on the ratty, old couch that had become a Ladies' Room landmark, April comforted herself with an awareness of the success of the group. Women came and went, according to their needs, but most of the original group remained. April's "leadership" had ceased to be necessary for some months. The group thrived and grew on the unguided camaraderie of its members.

"I read your story yesterday," Mo said. "Ten cars derailed and one person killed."

"Yeah, and it's like pulling crocodile teeth to get information from the railroad," April responded.

Mo dropped to a seat beside April. "Sooooo, meet any nice small-town girls just dying to come out of the closet?"

"You're sick, Thompson. Only you'd think of that in the middle of a train wreck," April responded. "The only people I met were a state trooper with bad breath and a motel clerk that has more hair than sense, and he's going bald."

"What about the waitress at the coffee shop?" Mo asked.

"She was in her sixties and carried a picture of her great-grandson."

"Bummer," Mo responded.

"The best part of the trip was…" April's sentence ended abruptly as Sophia appeared in the doorway.

"Hi," April greeted. Her gaze focused on the dark-haired lawyer.

"*Hola*," Sophia responded. The round of greetings continued as the group welcomed the newcomer. Sophia smiled her acknowledgment, but there was a subdued shyness unusual in the confident professional. She slipped quietly to a seat across from April.

"You were saying?" Mo asked, leaning toward her friend.

"What?"

"No fair, I asked first," Mo responded.

April chewed at her lower lip, trying to recall the earlier conversation. "I haven't a clue what you're talking about."

Johnnie snorted with pseudo humor. "Something make you forget what you were saying, honey?" April's old friend left her position behind the couch, abandoning April's shoulder massage, and moved to the now full refreshment table.

"Looks that way," April answered. "Was I saying something?"

Mo gave a short, barking laugh and leaned forward, facing Sophia. "You have the same effect when you arrive in the courtroom?" she asked. Sophia blushed as Mo returned her attention to April. "Darned if you didn't leave us hanging. You were just telling us what you thought was the best part of your trip."

April looked blankly into thin air. "I was? Heck, and I didn't think there was anything good about my trip." April looked toward Sophia. "Not the best of times to be leaving home, either."

Johnnie dropped a dish noisily. Two chocolate chip cookies rolled to the floor.

"Watch it, Johnnie!" Billboard called from across the room where she'd been discussing basketball scores. "Those are Allison's homemade cookies. You might as well throw away gold."

"Don't worry," Allison said, "I made an extra dozen, just for you Billboard."

The sorority lady joined in the conversation, waving a delicate hand sporting pink fingernail polish. "I've been meaning to ask, why do they call you Billboard?"

"Because of how she hits a softball," Mo answered.

A furrow of confusion creased the sorority lady's brow. "You hit a softball with a billboard? Is that another name for a bat?"

Laughter rippled through the room, almost covering the sound of breaking glass from the bar below. Almost, but not quite. The room grew silent as those present strained to hear.

"You all hear that?" Johnnie asked.

As though in answer, the crash of breaking furniture and the shouts of angry male voices drifted through the floor from the bar below.

"What the hell was that?" Mo demanded.

April looked around and saw her own wide-eyed shock reflected on the faces surrounding her. Without hesitation, April rushed for the door and pounded down the stairs to the Pink Triangle. The herd of women rushed with her down the steps and through the back door of the bar. April burst through the door and paused in shock. The other women, straining to see inside, jostled her forward.

Tandy sat crumpled on the floor near the bar, her face bruised and bleeding and she held her left arm tenderly with her right hand. Two men stood over her, their faces distorted by nylon stockings over their heads. One held a baseball bat threateningly over his head.

"You are an abomination before the Lord!" The fat belly of the second man jiggled, as he shouted, a Bible held like a weapon before him. He wore a black turtleneck and too-new jeans, still stiff and creased, the impromptu costume of this inexperienced commando. "You..." he leaned toward Tandy, the venom in his voice growing in strength. "...you dare create this den of iniquity...preying on the weaknesses of those devils living an unnatural life."

April took in the rest of the room as his tirade continued. Bart lay unconscious near the dance floor, and two more men—wearing the same uniform of nylon stocking, turtle necks and jeans—were working up a sweat, breaking chairs and tables with sledge hammer and ax.

Fury, unlike any April had ever known, boiled at her toes and coursed up her body, erupting in volcanic rage.

"What the fuck do you think you're doing?" April's shout cut off all motion in the room. A visible change rippled through the men, as they looked up to see the mob of women crowded near the back door. The belly of the fat man continued to jiggle, no longer with his shouts, but now with fear.

Two men gathered their courage and faced the women with their sledgehammer and ax. April felt a jostle ripple through the women behind her, just before she felt a baseball bat thrust into her hand. She looked to each side to see Mo, Billboard, and Alli taking stances beside her, each holding a bat from the equipment bag Mo always carried in the trunk of her car. From the corner of her eye, she saw some of the other women rummaging through the wreckage to retrieve table and chair legs as impromptu weapons.

"Let's go!" the fat man squeaked, as he led a hasty retreat out the front door. April and her group hesitated momentarily, prepared for a fight not a retreat. It was enough for the four men to get the head-start they needed. April led the group that ran after them, and arrived just as the four men jumped into a blue van (the license plate predictably missing). The van was rolling before the last man was completely inside. In desperation, Billboard launched her bat toward the van, using all the strength that made her the homerun champ of Amber. The bat smashed the back window of the van before clanking to the pavement.

"God damn, sons of bitches!" Billboard screamed, waving her arms as though she wished she had another bat to throw.

After the van squealed around the corner, the group of women turned to each other, expressing their anger and dithering, not knowing whether to pursue the van or return to the Pink Triangle. The immediate wash of anger had passed for April, and she felt numb with disbelief. Between the demands of covering the train wreck and the attack on one of her sacred places, April struggled to make her brain function.

"*Tandy!*" April yelled, abruptly remembering her injured friend. She rushed inside and found Sophia and Stella tending to Tandy where she still rested on the floor and to a now conscious Bart. Stella struggled to hold him down as he held a rag to his bleeding forehead and waved his arms in a staccato motion that matched the oaths with which he filled the air. April dropped to her knees by her old friend.

"You okay, Tandy?"

"Been better, but I'll live."

April looked at her friend's obviously broken arm. "Did anyone call an ambulance? The police?"

"*Sí, mija.* They're on their way," Sophia answered.

"Somebody needs to call, Sharon," April said, thinking of Tandy's lover. She started to rise when she felt Mo's hand push her back down.

"I'll do it," Mo said. "You stay with Tandy." Mo walked away as she pulled a cell phone from her pocket.

April placed her hand on Bart's shoulder. "Calm down buddy. Save your energy for the next fight."

The energy left him, and Bart collapsed against the bar, in tears. "I tried, Tandy. I didn't want them to hurt you or the Pink Triangle. I'm sorry."

"Sorry for what? You put up a good fight, fella. Be proud of yourself," Tandy said. She barked a humorless laugh and nodded her head toward her injured arm. "Did better than me. That fellow put me down with one pop of that hammer. Sure would have liked to get my hands on Fatso, though."

"Any idea who they were?" April asked.

"Not a clue. Religious types by the sound of it. Fatso was spouting scripture and where else would a bunch of tough guys take orders from the likes of him?" Tandy answered.

"He the boss?"

"Sounded like it to me."

The sound of nearby sirens brought the conversation to a halt. All but a dedicated few from the Ladies' Room abruptly disappeared. In conservative Amber, most gays were more willing to face a barroom riot than have their names on a police report from a fight in a gay bar. April suggested that Sophia leave and was greeted with the fiery light of anger in the attorney's eyes.

"I'll not run away," Sophia answered.

The EMTs treated Bart and Tandy, including splinting Tandy's arm, before loading them in the ambulance and hauling them to the hospital. Tandy asked that they take them to St. Anthony's, knowing that Sharon was working the pediatrics wing. April called the hospital after they left, telling Sharon they were on their way. The police were already questioning witnesses before April was off the phone. She had started toward where one uniformed officer was taking notes from the accounts of Sophia and Stella when she felt Sandy's hand on her arm. She turned to face the cowgirl.

"What's up?" April asked.

"I think there's something you should hear." Sandy said, as she directed April toward a dark corner of the bar, one where a table and chairs still stood intact. She could see Alli and Judy, the cowhand from the Four Sixes, comforting a hunched figure. As April drew closer, she saw that the distraught girl was Terry, the quiet young woman who had so moved the first session of the Ladies' Room.

April sat across from the young woman. "It's over Terry. Don't worry, we're all here, and you're safe."

Terry lifted her face and the look in her eyes made April's heart pause in her chest. It wasn't fear she saw there. It was hate...pure, cold, and down to the soul.

"It was him," Terry said.

"Who?"

"The preacher."

"You mean Fatso?"

"Yes," Terry hissed.

"Who is he?"

"Reverend Ralph Thomas," Terry answered, biting at every word. "The man who killed Marilyn."

"Are you sure it was him?"

"Yes."

April looked to locate an officer. "Wait here. You need to tell the police."

⁂

April collapsed on the couch. She buried her face in her hands and used the palms to rub at her eyes in a vain attempt to force away the exhaustion and frustration that made her eyes gritty and burning.

"It's been one helluva day," April said.

Sophia grasped one of April's wrists and gently pulled her hand from her face. She handed April a cold glass of prickly pear tea. April downed it in one glorious swallow.

"I swear this stuff has healing properties," April said.

"My grandmother swore by it."

April was aware of Sophia's closeness as they sat side by side on Sophia's overstuffed couch. In its own way, the fear she felt equaled that of facing Tandy's attackers at the Pink Triangle.

"Thank you for driving me home," Sophia said.

"Why in the world did you have your sister drop you off instead of bringing your car to the Ladies' Room?"

Sophia smiled, shyly. "Do you want the truth or the excuse?"

April directed a mock glare at Sophia. "I'm a

reporter. What do you think?"

"The truth then." Sophia took a deep breath. "I wanted you to drive me home."

The ice in April's glass clinked against the sides so that April could not hide the shaking of her hand. She placed the glass on the coffee table in an efficient, but graceless, motion.

"Why?"

Sophia leaned close, placing her hand under April's chin, pulling April's face toward her own. Her answer was a kiss…a sweet, long kiss that slowly eased the tension in both women. April moved, placing her arms around the small, dark woman, and Sophia subtly eased her body against April until they were molded as one. The kiss continued, gradually increasing in passion as the two women gained confidence in what the other felt. April moaned and buried her face in Sophia's shoulder, holding her even more tightly than before. Sophia felt something happen as April let go of the determination that had carried her through the difficulties of the past two days. The Latina grasped the other woman tightly, instinctively feeling her need for comfort. Even at that, Sophia was surprised at the warm dampness of tears against her shoulder.

"*Que pasa, mí preciosa?* What's wrong, my precious?"

April leaned back, wiping her eyes on her sleeve. "Not sure. Just…just too much to think and feel, I guess."

Sophia pulled away. "Do you want me to leave you al—?"

April's hand moved so quickly that Sophia was unprepared for the certainty of the grip on her shoulder. "Don't you dare!" April laughed. "Sophia, being kept from you all day yesterday and today is a good deal of what's turned me into an emotional basket case."

"That and tonight."

April's smile disappeared, and her mouth took on a hard line. "Yes, and tonight. My God, those guys…" April's voice quavered, "…those guys might have killed Tandy if we hadn't interrupted."

Sophia shushed April and used delicate fingers to brush April's hair from her face. "Enough for tonight, *querida*. Rest and relax. Besides, it has been difficult for me, too, not being with you since our last meeting. There is something you must know, and I don't think I am willing to delay any longer."

"Do you know what you want?" April asked.

"Yes," Sophia answered as she kissed April again, long and slow.

The frustration of the train wreck, the fear and anger of the attack on the Pink Triangle, April forgot them all as she tasted Sophia's tongue on her own. She enjoyed the kiss, savored the sensuality and gentleness, even as she felt the intensity of the moment increase. Sophia pushed away from April and looked at her with eyes black with passion.

"I have always wanted to…" Sophia's hands finished the sentence, as she tugged at the buttons on April's shirt, finally gaining access to the breasts beneath. Sophia's hand shook as she touched the soft skin, tentatively at first, but more aggressively as she enjoyed what she felt. April moaned and pushed against the questing fingers. She pulled Sophia closer and nibbled the base of the Latina's neck, pushing aside the lengths of dark hair.

"*Querida*, they feel wonderful. Better than I ever

dreamed." Sophia whispered against April's ear.

April gave a throaty laugh, quiet in the intimacy they now felt. "This isn't what I planned for us...not for the first time."

"You planned?" Sophia teased.

A blush colored April's cheeks. "Yes, I planned... or perhaps I should say hoped."

"It is enough for me that I am finally here with you."

April gently touched the softness of Sophia's face. "And I cannot tell you how happy I am to be here." She laughed. "But this has been one of the longest days of my life. I'm dirty and sweaty. I look a mess, and I bet I taste salty."

Sophia licked playfully at April's exposed chest and laughed when April inhaled with the suddenness of the sensation. "Yes, you do. What of it?"

"I need a shower."

"I will let you shower under one condition."

"Yes?"

"That you stay the night with me."

April felt unexpected tears spring to her eyes. "Nothing would please me more."

Sophia rose in a single, fluid motion, pulling April to her feet along with her. "I'll show you where everything is. While you shower I'll..." Sophia hesitated.

April smiled. "Slip into something more comfortable?" They both laughed.

Not since her tour on the USS Lexington had April showered so quickly. She spent the few minutes under the water half hoping Sophia would join her and half hoping her soon-to-be lover would wait. There was still an awkwardness between them, the desire for each other without the knowledge of each other. When she stepped out of the shower, April found a soft towel and warm robe waiting for her on the bathroom counter. She took a deep breath and opened the bathroom door. Whisps of steam preceded her into the master bedroom, adding an ethereal look to the image before her. April paused, making herself believe the sight of Sophia, dark hair splayed on the pillow, framing her face and accenting the twinkle of excitement in her dark eyes.

April stepped forward. The shy smile on Sophia's face was reflected on her own as April crawled beneath the covers, still wearing the robe. Sophia welcomed her with open arms, pausing to pull at the tie on April's robe.

"I don't think you'll need this," Sophia laughed as she pulled the robe away.

A momentary vulnerability almost overcame April as she was acutely aware of her nakedness beside Sophia in her silk nightgown. The vulnerability was brief as April became acutely aware of the feel of that nightgown…and of the woman beneath. Sophia kissed her with an intensity that spoke of passion postponed, and even as she returned the kiss with equal pleasure, April realized her surprise at Sophia's aggression, her willingness to lead the way in what they now shared. No sooner had April noted her own surprise than Sophia's aggression disappeared and there was an air of shyness as Sophia buried her face in April's neck.

"I want this," Sophia mumbled.

"So do I," April answered, running her fingers gently along Sophia's silk-clad back.

"I'm frightened," Sophia responded.

April held the Latina tightly against her. "There's

no need to be afraid. I won't hurt you."

"I know." Sophia leaned back and looked into her lover's eyes. "But I don't know what to do."

April chuckled and a twinkle filled her gaze. "Anything you want to do."

Sophia smiled, relaxing slightly. "I have no lack of imagination, but...but...actually doing what I imagine..."

"Is frightening?"

"Yes."

April stroked Sophia's cheek and stared at the other woman with gentle longing. "Then I guess I'll just have to go first."

A kiss of even greater intensity than those that preceded halted all conversation. When April's mouth finally left Sophia's, it was only to move downward, nibbling at Sophia's neck and on to the nipples now erect beneath the silk. Uncaring, April left a dark wet patch on the silk as she played her tongue over each nipple. Sophia moaned as she thrust her body even closer to April. In a joint movement that felt like a dance, the two women worked together to pull Sophia's nightgown over her head.

April continued to move lips, teeth, and tongue over Sophia's body, down her stomach and chest, and along her thighs. As her mouth worked, her fingers traced an unruly pattern on Sophia's back, buttocks, and legs, causing the darker woman to moan, move, and even shake with a growing passion. Finally, April reached her destination. Sophia grew momentarily still as April nestled between her legs and began to feed. With a hunger of longing, April fed on Sophia's pleasure. As that pleasure grew, April's efforts and her own passion, increased as she continued to nurture Sophia's sexual center. When Sophia finally cried out, her whole body tensing in climax, April felt disappointment as Sophia pulled away, unable to handle any more stimulation.

"Come to me," Sophia moaned, still shaking from her experience.

April moved within the circle of Sophia's arms and they lay against each other.

"I don't think this will be a day either of us will forget," April said.

"Most certainly not."

For a moment, April's mind drifted from her immediate pleasure. "We still have to do something about Tandy and the good Reverend Thomas."

Sophia shushed her lover. "*Mañana Querida.* And for now..." Sophia paused to kiss her lover, "... it is my turn."

April's body quivered in anticipation.

Chapter Ten

What do you mean there's nothing you can do?" April demanded of the police detective.

"I meant just that, Sims. Right now, there's nothing we can do," Sergeant Folkers responded.

"But you've got an eyewitness."

"No Sims. We've got an ear witness. Your friend only recognized Thomas's voice. She never got a look at his face."

"Come on, Frank. You know good and well it was him that led his good Christian coalition in attacking Tandy and her bar," April said.

The detective leaned across the table, an air of threat shadowing his friendly demeanor. "Listen, Sims. Just because it's your friend doesn't mean you can forget what you know about how things work. You're a reporter. You've seen enough of this stuff. It doesn't matter what I know. What matters is what I can prove."

April's eyes narrowed and she looked closely at this man she'd known for so many years. "Tell me Frank. If the Pink Triangle weren't a gay bar, would you take it to the D.A.?"

The man pushed back his chair and contemplated his fingertips. "Don't know. Maybe."

"Tell me Frank. Had you figured me out?"

The detective half barked a laugh. "Come on,

Sims. The rainbow bumper sticker on your car is a dead giveaway."

"You know about the rainbow?"

The sergeant directed a look at April that told her he wouldn't honor that question with an answer.

"Okay, then. It's never bothered you to work with me."

"Hell, no. You can be tough, but you got sense." Folkers chewed his lip. "A good cop is out to protect the good guys and get the bad guys." The man nodded and gave April a tired smile. "You'd make a good cop."

The fire in April's eyes punctuated her next question. "Can you tell me that the gay issue isn't affecting how you handle this case?"

The man laughed. "Of course it is."

April leaned back, surprised. "Explain."

"Any cop knows that any crime against a queer—don't mean for the word to offend you, but it's the way some folks think—has to be twice as bad, and you have to work twice as hard to prove it before a jury will convict. Especially around here. Jesus, Sims, we're in the middle of the damn Bible belt." The officer sighed in frustration. "If I arrest some preacher for trashing a gay bar, some folks would think he was a hero. It would be a public affairs nightmare for the whole department. It ain't fair, Sims, but that's the way it is."

"So you'll do nothing," April responded.

"Didn't say that. We'll be watching him. We'll be watching the Pink Triangle. If we can get good, hard evidence, I'll arrest the fat bugger and to hell with the public's response."

April's shoulders slumped. "I guess that's the best we can hope for."

Folkers placed his hand on April's arm. "You've

got a cool head, Sims, and a good heart. If you let anyone in the department know I told you this, I'll deny it, but we leak information to you now and again just because we want to hear what you think. Truth is, lady, I'd claim you for a partner any day." The detective stood over the table and used his fist to thump April on the upper arm. "And I don't let the bad guys fuck with my partners. Not if I can help it." The sergeant nodded once and was out the door of the newspaper's conference room before April could respond.

April wallowed in a stunned sense of pleased surprise at the sergeant's admiration combined with a deep disappointment that she wouldn't be writing of Reverend Ralph Thomas's arrest for the evening paper. She sat quietly, gathering her thoughts. Sam Trimble, the managing editor, and Kate Stevens, the city editor appeared in the doorway. Without invitation, they found empty seats at the table.

"What did he say?" Sam asked.

"Until we have hard evidence, we're shit out of luck and Reverend Thomas stays free," April answered.

Sam's face reddened. "Just because a crime's against an unpopular subpopulation, that's no reason for the police not to do their job."

April sighed. "Frank's doing his best, but he did tell me the facts of life. The police are going to be watching for evidence and trying to protect Tandy and the Pink Triangle, but that's it. The crime has to be bad, and the evidence has to be strong, before they'll press charges for a gay-related hate crime."

Kate banged her fist against the table in an uncharacteristic show of violence. "It's not fair!"

April raised one eyebrow and looked at her boss. "Kate, we're journalists. Isn't that one of the basic precepts from Journalism 101? Life isn't fair."

Sam leaned forward, both hands flat against the table. "And all my years in the business, I've never lost the excitement of knowing that part of our job is striving to make life just a little fairer."

Kate laughed. "The police may not be able to do much, but maybe we can."

"What?" April asked. "They're not pressing charges. The most I can report is vandalism and assault by unknown assailants at a bar on Sixth Street called the Pink Triangle."

Sam leaned back, and the chair protested with a frightening creak. "I know Kate and I are the editors here, but you're more than just a reporter on a story for this one. These are your people and your cause." At his words April felt an internal fire redden her face. "I think I'm going to leave this call up to you. What do we do?"

April sat deep in thought. "You know, Sam. When someone has you in a corner with no choice but to fight, sometimes the only plan is to use their own weapon against them."

"Yeah, so?" Sam responded.

"Reverend Thomas has been making good use of our letters to the editor, hasn't he?"

Kate shuddered. "People like him almost make me regret the First Amendment." Sam and April looked at their fellow journalist in shock. "Almost, but not quiet," Kate clarified.

"Kate, you mind if one of your reporters changes hats and writes an editorial?" April asked. "The police may think the public doesn't believe that gays are human with the rights that go with being human, but I have more faith in people than that."

Sam and Kate looked at each other and smiled. "I think that sounds like an excellent idea."

❧ ❧ ❧ ❧

Amber Daily News – Editorial
Is Jesus Violent?
By April Sims, staff writer

The man spouted scripture, while his companions used baseball bats and sledge hammers to give two of my friends concussions and broke one of their arms so badly she needed surgery. Last Tuesday night, they trashed the Pink Triangle, a bar a dear friend of mine has run for over twenty years. While they beat, bashed, and battered flesh, metal, glass, and wood, they kept shouting about Jesus and the judgement of God. It was news to me, but I guess Jesus likes violence. These men seemed to think so.

As a news reporter, I cover acts of violence all the time, and I strive to cover the facts, that which can be proven from objective documentation. I didn't have to go far for this story. I saw it with my own eyes. I was nearby with a group of friends when we heard the shouts and the mayhem. Four men did the dirty deed. They ran when we arrived and the numbers were no longer in their favor.

Sure, their faces were contorted behind nylon stockings, and the old van was without a license plate as they fled from the Pink Triangle. One of my friends managed to break out the van's back window, before they were out of range, but other than the broken glass, it would be difficult to identify either the men or their vehicle. No, we can't swear to it, but we're pretty sure who they were. It's not the first time one particular minister in one particular church has expressed his hatred for people like me.

I'm a lesbian. The Pink Triangle is a well-known gathering place for those of us who know that our orientation is to bond with and love members of our own gender. We are who we are, and I, for one, offer no apology nor feel any shame for just being who I am. A handful of men proved Tuesday night that they think being a homosexual means deserving to be a victim of violence. I suspect, they believe they will be immune from their actions because "everyone" agrees with their "Godly" point of view.

I know better.

I live and work with a wide range of people, every day. I don't wave a rainbow flag – well, not very often anyway, but I don't hide who I am. My neighbors, my coworkers, my mechanic, my doctor, and even friends from the church I attend now and again, they treat me with dignity, respect, and even love.

There are those of you out there who know the masked, scripture-spouting preacher who led the raid on the Pink Triangle. I can't tell him face to face, so I hope you'll deliver this message.

I don't believe Jesus likes violence. I am personally convinced that the majority of the people of Amber would not condone his actions nor the actions of the men who helped him. The police are looking for them now. What they did was a crime against the people they damaged, against the state, and, although it isn't mine to judge, perhaps against God himself, who or whatever that may be.

Hate crimes hurt everyone, not just the direct victims of those crimes. Readers, if you know those who commit or plan such crimes, and do or say nothing, you are a party to the damage they do. We already know of at least one suicide tied directly to one local minister's lesson of hatred toward homosexuals. Please, if there is anything any of you can do to prevent another crime, perhaps another death, do it.

❧ ❧ ❧ ❧

Sophia waited just inside the entrance to the hospital. As April drove past, looking for a parking place, she could see anger behind the practiced poise of the Latina's facial expression. April jogged from the parking lot to the hospital, anxious to see the woman who was now her lover. The anger disappeared from Sophia's eyes, as April approached, and there was a hidden heat to their brief, public embrace.

"*Hola, mí amora,*" Sophia whispered to April in their moment of closeness. April blushed and hoped Sophia could see in her eyes the intense pleasure April felt at just being near her.

"Have you already been up?" April asked.

"No, I arrived not long before you." The angry crease returned between Sophia's eyebrows as they walked toward the elevator. "I was detained in court."

"Did you have any luck with a restraining order?"

"No. Judge Smithson is just as reluctant as your Sergeant Folkers to accuse a minister of attacking a group of homosexuals."

"Stinks, doesn't it?"

Sophia mumbled a string of Spanish April didn't understand. The one word she did comprehend was one she'd never learned in the classroom. She'd first seen it spray painted on a wall in the barrio. The elevator door opened, and they stepped inside.

Tandy was sitting in bed, glaring at the talk show playing on the television suspended on the wall across from her hospital bed. Sharon read quietly in a recliner beside the bed.

"My, my, don't you look happy?" April said.

Tandy jabbed a stubby finger at the TV remote, silencing the irritating boom of the television. "I'm fine, and there's work to do. I don't know why I'm still in the hospital."

Sharon lowered her novel and looked toward the visitors. "She is not a good patient," Sharon sighed.

"Glad she's not on your ward?" April asked.

"Glad isn't the word. She's been the kind of patient that makes me want to look for longer needles."

Tandy glared at her lover. When Sharon glared back, Tandy lowered her gaze. "Well, hell! I don't mean to be a grouch, but I have a bar to run. I know I won't be able to open tonight, but I have regular folks on Thursday nights, and I want them to know that the Pink Triangle's not going to close because of some big-mouthed preacher and his bunch of masked cowards."

"Honey, they want to keep you under observation for one more night. Besides the concussion, they'll x-ray your arm again tomorrow to ensure that it's set properly."

Tandy's air of anger eased as she studied April and Sophia. A mischievous smile teased at her lips, as she looked from April to Sophia and back again. "April, my friend, you're looking good, considering all the trauma."

April blushed, knowing that her old friend saw all. "All things considered, life's not bad." Sophia stood very still displaying uncharacteristic shyness. April stepped closer, placing her arm around Sophia's waist, attempting to communicate that Sophia truly belonged.

"Welcome to the family, Sophia," Sharon said. She stood and gave Sophia a warm hug.

All of Tandy's earlier bruskness evaporated. "Sophia, our April here's been alone for a long time. I can't tell you how glad I am to see the twinkle back in her eye."

"And a shiny glow to my coat," April teased.

Sophia laughed. "What am I, dog food?"

April looked tenderly at Sophia. "More like ambrosia."

"Hot ziggidy damn! She's got it bad," Tandy spouted.

Sharon swatted her lover with her paperback. *"Tandy!"*

Sophia reached for April's hand as they both laughed. "It's okay, Sharon," April responded. "Tandy's right. I got it bad."

Tenderly, Sophia touched April's face. "It's mutual."

"I take it this means we have a foursome for cards next Sunday?" Tandy asked.

April looked to Sophia. "What do you think?"

Sophia laughed. "Sounds like fun, but I must warn you, I play to win."

"Of course you do. You're an attorney aren't you?" Tandy responded.

Sharon sighed and dropped back into her recliner. "Don't worry. If any blood's shed, I'm a nurse."

April beamed a phony smile. "And I can write all about it in the paper."

"And I can pour enough drinks so that no one will give a damn anyway," Tandy added.

"Sounds like a plan to me," April said.

Sharon picked up the newspaper beside her. "It looks as if you've been busy," she said.

"Did you read the editorial?"

"We sure did," Tandy responded. "You got guts, my friend. But you keep your head low, you hear me?"

They only stayed a few more minutes. Their visit distracted her from her worries, but she tired rapidly. As April and Sophia said their farewells, Tandy eased back into the pillow, looking far more relaxed than she did when they'd first arrived. After a brief visit with Bart, also under observation for a concussion, April and Sophia left, agreeing to meet at April's house so that she could feed the dog and change before they both went to dinner.

The light on April's answering machine blinked like an epileptic stop light as Sophia followed her inside the house.

"Looks like a few folks read my editorial," April commented as she threw her notebook and the paper on the coffee table. Sophia stepped behind, placing her arms around her lover's waist and speaking with her cheek against April's back.

"This may not be pleasant, *mija*," Sophia said.

April grinned slyly and retrieved notebook and pen, handing both to Sophia. "Here, you take an inventory while I look after Nearly and change my clothes."

"Thank you for giving me such a pleasant task," Sophia responded wryly.

"Make sure you save all the messages. I may need to play them for the police," April instructed.

Sophia sat on the chair by the phone and punched play, as April made her way toward the back door to let Nearly in from the yard. Despite an effort not to listen, words like bitch, sinner, and damnation floated to April as she greeted her four-legged companion and then retreated to her room in the rear of the house. In fresh clothes and with newly cleaned teeth, she returned to the living room where Sophia was still hunched over the phone, taking notes. As April entered, she heard pleasant words from a gentle male voice telling how much he appreciated her courage.

"How'd it go?" April asked.

As the lengthy message continued, Sophia looked up to smile at her new lover. "It's about three to one in favor of your editorial, but the one-third are not pleasant people. Someone really must tell one gentleman that it's impossible to castrate a lesbian."

April whistled. "Jeez, glad I had a tough-skinned attorney to take messages for me."

"Why don't you have caller ID?"

"I think that I better buy a machine after dinner. I've already got the service with the phone company. I just never bothered to get the hardware."

They continued to converse as a beep marked the end of the message and a new voice started. Their conversation ended midsentence as the professional tones of a male voice identified himself. April knelt beside Sophia and hit the rewind button briefly, hitting near the beginning of the message.

"Hello, Miss Sims. I'm Alfred Jones, a member of the board at Reverend Ralph Thomas's church. I was distressed to learn of what happened at your friend's...establishment. It's urgent that I talk with you." Sophia scratched at the notepad, capturing the man's phone number.

They looked at each other, wide-eyed.

"I'd say this one merits a phone call," April said.

"I think you're right," Sophia answered.

Chapter Eleven

April leafed through a copy of *Outdoor Life*, dog-eared and out of season, as she sat in the waiting area of the real estate office. The choice had been between an ancient *Outdoor Life* and an impressive stack of *Reader's Digest*. April avoided *Reader's Digest,* They represented too many memories of too many waiting rooms, with every type of unpleasant experience on the other side of too many innocuous doors—dentists, doctors, counselors. April had long thought "waiting room" a misnomer. More like "anxiety room." Today was no exception. This could be a traumatic interview.

Alfred Jones knew she was there. She saw recognition in the man's eyes as soon as she entered the building. Cubicle offices for the firm's three agents surrounded the waiting area, but she hadn't needed to ask the secretary which one was Mr. Jones. As April entered the building, he looked through the picture window that separated his office from the waiting area. When they made eye contact, April felt the intensity of his gaze, a strange mixture of embarrassment and determination. In that brief moment, April identified Alfred Jones as a man determined to do the right thing. He nodded in recognition, not interrupting his session with the young couple sitting in front of his desk. April didn't even have time to finish the article on rock climbing, before she saw the young couple rise, while Alfred sent them on their way with a smile and a stack of freshly signed documents.

Mr. Jones smile lost a touch of its intensity as the couple exited through the front door, and he turned to face his next visitor. He stood inside his office doorway, visibly collecting his composure, as he repeatedly straightened the lapels of his jacket. April also noticed his nervous glance outside the plate glass window overlooking the parking lot. In that instant, she realized the risk this man dared.

"Are you April Sims?" he asked.

"Yes."

As a reflex, Jones reached for a handshake before his hand retreated to his suit pocket. April could see his hand fiddle nervously beneath the material. The movement was subtle, but it made April wonder if Alfred Jones had ever before knowingly conversed with a lesbian. He seemed to fear her, as though she carried a dreaded disease.

"I appreciate your coming to my office."

"Sounded important," April responded.

The man straightened his lapels and looked directly into April's eyes. "It is." Mr. Jones waved toward his office. "Won't you come in?"

April stepped inside and took a seat as Jones closed the door. He sat at his desk and played absently with an inexpensive pen blazoned with the name of his firm. The repeated click, click irritated April. She sat patiently, waiting for the man to initiate the conversation.

"I…I wanted to apologize," Jones said.

"For what?" April asked.

Three quick clicks on the pen reinforced April's awareness of the gentleman's difficulty with continuing the conversation. "Not all of us at New Life Ministries agree with Brother Thomas's views."

"I appreciate your courage in calling me. I don't imagine Ralph Thomas is very receptive to disagreement."

Jones's face reddened. "I supported Brother Thomas when we voted to call him as pastor. I'm growing to believe it was a serious mistake." The man cleared his throat. "Don't misunderstand. I don't agree with your…that is, I believe it's wrong to be a…"

"Homosexual," April said.

"Yes."

April shrugged. "I'd never deny anyone the right to their beliefs."

"Yet you continue to live a life that's evil," the man said, in a flash of anger.

A sad smile teased at April's eyes and lips. "Mr. Jones, I respect what you believe, but I don't believe as you do." She leaned forward, emphasizing her words. "Most gays have had to go through some pretty awful self-hate, because people like you tell us we're evil. I grew past that a long time ago. I'm at peace with myself and my God, and I don't need you to tell me what God thinks of me and my lifestyle."

"But the Bible says…"

"The Bible says, 'Judgement is mine, sayeth the Lord.' I have no problem at all waiting for God to pass judgement on my life." April pushed her hair away from her face in an irritated motion. "I wonder if Reverend Ralph Thomas could say the same."

A rapid percussion of clicks from the ballpoint pen indicated the depth of Alfred Jones's troubled thoughts. "I don't know," he responded softly. "I'm sorry, Miss Sims. What Brother Thomas and his followers did to your friend and her business was wrong."

"We agree on that."

"I will do what I can to persuade them not to resort to violence."

"Will you tell the police what you know?"

The pen started a rapid rendition of "Wipeout."

"No, I cannot condone what they did, but I understand their persecution of your lifestyle."

"Mr. Jones, they didn't break my lifestyle's arm or send my lifestyle to the hospital. That was Tandy Johnson, one of the finest women I've ever known."

Alfred Jones's face grew pale, and the click of the pen ceased. April had hit home.

"You're right," he said, so soft she could barely hear. "And I'm sorry. I feel responsible that I didn't stop them."

April sat in silence, studying the face of the man opposite her. His eyes were clear and deep. They were honest eyes. *If I ever buy a house, it will be from this man,* April thought.

"Don't beat yourself up, Mr. Jones. I didn't see you wielding an ax."

"Even so, I'm an elder in the church and past chairman of the board. I should have stopped it."

April leaned toward the man. "Mr. Jones, if you had seen it coming, I have no doubt that you would have done everything in your power to make sure your Brother Thomas and his crew never carried their persecution to the point of violence."

The man raised his head and looked directly into April's eyes. "I swear to you, I would have done my best, and I'll do my best to ensure it doesn't happen again."

There was no amusement in April's smile, but it was a sincere smile all the same. She stood and reached across the desk.

"Mr. Jones, I know you don't approve of lesbians, but, if you can bring yourself to do it, I'd be proud to shake your hand."

The man stood and accepted her offered hand. In the strength of their handshake, a bond was formed, a mutual respect. The tickle along the hairs at the back of her neck made April wonder if this bond wouldn't prove important.

❧❧❧❧

Slider sat on the hood of his battered Chevy, sipping on a soda from the nearby convenience store. He had that blankly studied expression April knew so well from assignments when Slider waited hours to get that one photo that would make the story. It was his, I'll-wait-in-this-other-universe-until-I'm-needed look. April walked toward him, as she left Alfred Jones's office.

"Thanks for the patience. That's what you get for thinking I need an escort," April said to her friend.

"I've heard your messages, honey. I'd like to see you stay alive through this deal," Slider answered. "You're not still set on going home, are you?"

"I've got to get some clothes, at least," April answered. A slow grin crossed her face. "Can't say that I object to a few days staying with Sophia. Nearly's already made himself at home in her backyard."

Slider laughed. "I won't be surprised if this becomes permanent."

They climbed into the Chevy, and Slider started

the drive to April's. "How'd it go with Jones?" he asked.

"He's a decent man. I don't agree with him, but I like and trust him."

"Nice to know the religious right has some pockets of decency."

They rode in companionable silence, each comfortable with their own thoughts. They'd learned the habitual rapport in the long hours of working together.

As they rounded the last corner to April's home, Slider's gasp jerked her gaze toward her duplex. Two-foot letters in red spray paint sprawled "Death to all abominations!!" across the front of her home.

"Jeez, Louise!!" Slider moaned.

"My landlord is really going to be pissed." April said.

They pulled to the curb and sat in shock. April rolled down her window as her neighbor walked out his front door and approached the Chevy. She waved absently at a man who had been her neighbor for three years. Hank and Sarah Smithson were good neighbors. The retired couple helped watch her house when she was out of town, and Sarah always made sure April got her share of pumpkin bread at Christmas and homemade apricot jelly in the summer. April was glad Hank was there to give support.

"So, where you been Ms. Abomination?"

"I stayed with a friend last night," April answered. "Looks like I missed all the fun."

"They weren't a noisy bunch, but Sarah did get up in the night to go to the bathroom and noticed a dark van parked across the street. We've already called the police. They looked around to see if your place had been burglarized, but said it still looked secure. They want you to call them." Hank rummaged in his shirt pocket and pulled out a business card. "You're supposed to call a Sergeant Folkers." He offered the card to April.

"Keep the card. I know Frank. His might be a handy number for you to keep around the house."

"We were worried about Nearly," Hank said.

"He's still over at my friend's house."

Hank's face showed visible relief. He looked back toward the house and the message scrawled across the front. "Neighbor, looks like you've had quite an initiation to editorial writing."

"Guess you think I should have stuck with news and feature," April responded.

A slow smile teased at the edge of her neighbor's lips. "Read like a pretty good piece to me."

April licked dry lips. "Hank, did you and Sarah...? Did you know that...?"

Hank laughed. "April, you're the best neighbor on the block. Your personal life is your own business."

The old car door screeched, as April pushed it open so she could step out and give her neighbor a hug. "Thanks for everything, Hank."

"Just being neighborly," the man answered, his face colored with a pleased blush. He motioned toward the graffiti. "You know, it'd probably be a good idea for you just to stay with that friend for a few days."

"That's what I'm planning. Slider brought me over to pick up clothes and stuff."

The man scratched at his beard. "We'll call the police if we see anyone around your place."

"You and Sarah are the best, Hank."

A twinkle lightened the man's eyes. "And don't

you forget it. I'm just glad you and Nearly are safe."

Slider insisted on entering the house first, his hand under his jean jacket, placed conveniently on the five-shot .38 he insisted on carrying while serving as April's self-appointed bodyguard. April teased him for his dramatics, but was secretly relieved. She checked the house and called Frank Folkers to let him know that no one had meddled inside the house. Their conversation was short since he already had the background. She started to tell him where she'd be staying, but he interrupted and told her to call him later. It was then that April realized just how serious the sergeant was about the case. He didn't want to risk any form of illegal phone tap. A quick phone call to her landlord advised the woman of the vandalism. It didn't take long for April to pack a bag and her briefcase. In less than an hour, April was locking the door behind her while Slider loaded her bags into the trunk of his car.

April breathed the proverbial sigh of relief as Slider started the car and pulled from the curb. For the first few blocks, April watched closely for any sign of a following car. She finally shook her head and laughed.

"I'm getting downright paranoid."

"Good, maybe you'll stay alive that way," Slider responded. "These are some sick folks we're dealing with."

"Maybe, and maybe their need to be right is just a little too strong."

"To Sophia's?" Slider asked.

"Wait a minute. Tandy got out of the hospital yesterday. I'll bet money she's at the bar. Let's go check on her."

As April predicted, Tandy's car was parked in its

usual spot beside the Pink Triangle. Tandy's string of curses at the cast on her arm greeted April and Slider as they entered the bar. Tandy awkwardly struggled with polishing glasses as they walked inside.

"Nice to see that you've gotten back your cheerful disposition," April said to her friend.

"I'd just as soon have full use of both arms."

April hopped to a seat on the top of the bar and kissed her old friend on the top of the head. "I'm just glad to have you out of the hospital and home."

"Ditto," Slider added.

Tandy set a half-polished glass on the bar. "Me too."

April and Slider looked around the room. "Not bad, considering how they trashed the place," Slider commented. Concerned community members had worked together to repair or replace every broken chair or table. They'd cleaned up every sliver of glass and drop of liquor from broken bottles, and new bottles now filled the shelves behind the bar. All in all, the place looked cleaner than April had ever seen it.

"Looks like the gang really came through," April said.

Tears teased at Tandy's eyes. "Damn right, they did."

Slider leaned across the bar and slapped Tandy playfully on the arm. "Say, is it too early in the day for a man to talk you out of a Coke?"

"Seeing as how you're in good company, I guess I could manage," Tandy answered.

Tandy poured sodas for both her friends, and Slider and April began telling the tale of April's graffittied house, when a stranger appeared in the doorway, silhouetted in the sunlight. The three could see the darkened form of a woman.

"I'm sorry, but the bar's not open yet," Tandy called.

"I know," a pleasant, husky voice responded. "I'm looking for April Sims."

In reflex, Slider reached inside his jacket, just then remembering the empty holster. He'd left the pistol in the car before entering the bar.

"I'm April Sims," April said.

The figure stepped into the bar. As she stepped out of the sunlight, April got a clear look at the woman. *That's really good drag*, April thought. She watched the practiced, ultra-feminine step of the male-to-female transgendered woman cross the bar toward her. She was dressed in the sleek lines of a green business suit, accented by matching purse and pumps with four-inch heels that brought her height to well over six feet. April studied her immaculately coiffed hair and could see no signs of a wig. It was a sure sign of a serious transsexual. She grew, cut, and styled her own hair to be an attractive woman. April believed that here was a woman trapped in a man's body. Watching her regal movements gave April a new appreciation for the term "queen."

"Can we talk in private?" the stranger asked in the practiced, husky tones of a deep-voiced woman.

"Sure."

April left the bar, and they walked to a corner table while Tandy and Slider watched their every step. The woman sat gracefully in a chair opposite April.

"How can I help you?" April asked.

"I read your editorial."

"You and half the world."

"I admire your courage, and I'd like to help," she

said.

"I appreciate any help I can get. What do you suggest?"

The woman took a deep breath. "My name is Adora, and I live in Dallas. I visit Amber regularly to work with a few…clients." April listened, not wanting to know her profession. "Although he's been a regular customer, there's one gentleman that I'd really rather not serve."

"Who is that?" April asked.

"Ralph Thomas."

April felt a flash of hope, confirmation of her instincts concerning the good Reverend Thomas. "I guess I have to ask how you work with him."

A deep laugh was accented by a gentle gesture as the individual flipped her hair back from her face. "I believe this will explain everything." The queen reached into her purse and pulled out a brown envelope, handing it to April. As April pulled a nine-by-ten photo from the paper, she gasped. The photo showed a graphic scene of a naked Ralph Thomas having anal sex with the transsexual woman sitting opposite her. In the photo, the woman's face was turned so that she would be difficult to identify. Embarrassed, April threw the envelope on top of the photo.

"That's certainly…interesting. I'm sure Reverend Thomas's congregation would be especially surprised."

The woman leaned forward with a death grip on April's forearm. "You've got to stop him," she hissed.

"I'm trying."

"Use this photo if you need, but stop him."

April pulled her arm free, a little frightened by the intensity. "I don't understand. Is this how you feel about most of your clients?"

"Not at all. Most of my men are truly wonderful. I love my work. You don't understand."

"Then help me."

The woman leaned forward again, lowering her voice to a whisper. "I'm just an occasional distraction for Ralph. I'm not what he really likes."

"His congregation thinks he really goes for his wife."

"His wife is a well-trained rag doll. He's beaten her down to nothing, literally."

"So what does he like?" April asked.

The woman leaned toward her again, fire in her eyes. "He likes boys, very young boys."

April felt nauseated.

Chapter Twelve

The office was much the same as her first visit, but April felt a sincerity in Alfred Jones's handshake. There was a trust, a mutual respect between them. As a journalist, April knew that feeling, the confidence that even if they dealt from opposite sides of the fence, this man would be honest and honorable. A sense of disgust plagued her as April remembered the purpose of her visit.

"I'm surprised you called so soon after our meeting," Mr. Jones said, as he offered her a seat in his inner office.

"There have been some new…developments, and I think you have a right to know."

Jones's brows creased. "I don't understand." An edge of concern filled his voice. "Has there been more violence? I spoke with the board and in the men's group, and I felt certain…"

"No violence. It's something different," April said.

"Yes?"

A long silence filled the room. "Go on, I'm listening," the man prompted.

April rubbed at her eyes, wondering how to proceed. "Mr. Jones, how many young boys do you have in your church?"

"Why do you ask?" Jones responded, a note of caution in his voice. April regretted the loss of trust.

"I'm just not sure that you…I wouldn't suggest…"

April sighed. "I don't think Reverend Thomas should be around children, especially boys."

Jones's face flushed with anger. "Listen here, young woman. I regret the violence to your friend and her business, but I'll not permit slander against my own minister."

April leaned toward the desk. "Believe me, Mr. Jones. I'm not just here to spread vicious rumors. Evidence came to me that the boys in your church may be in real danger."

"I'll not simply take your word for that. Where is this 'evidence' against a God-fearing man?"

April's fingers played over the brown envelope in her hand. It held a copy of the original photo of Thomas and Adora. The police now had the original, but she'd had Slider scan a copy before she took it to Sgt. Folkers and told him Adora's tale. She felt slimed, hating herself for the effect her next action would have on the man in front of her. She tossed the envelope across the desk and watched as Jones opened the clasp and pulled out the picture.

His face went white, then green. He dropped the photo and wiped his hands against his jacket.

"It must be a forgery," he almost whispered.

"It's not. The police already ran a computer analysis. It's really him doing what it really looks like he's doing," April said.

Jones took a handkerchief from his jacket and wiped his sweating brow. April reached across the desk, replacing the picture to the envelope and committing a simple act of mercy in removing it from the man's sight.

"Will the police…will they confirm that?" Jones asked.

"Yes. You can call Sergeant Folkers at headquarters."

"I will."

The man cleared his throat several times. Even at that, his voice was weak as he continued. "Why do you think…what did you say about…boys?"

"The…other person in the photo came to see me. She asked me to stop Ralph Thomas because Reverend Thomas prefers young boys."

Jones's face made another transition to an almost lifeless white with splotches of green. April eyed the couch against the wall.

"Mr. Jones, I really think you need to lie down. Can I get you some water?"

"Perhaps I should," he mumbled.

April helped him to the couch. Once he was prone, she took a cup from his desk and returned with water from the cooler in the hallway. He sipped tentatively at the water.

"Why do people always go for water if someone's faint?" he asked.

April laughed lightly. "Don't know. Maybe it's to give people something to do so they won't hover, sucking up all the air." April was relieved. His color looked slightly better.

"Do you…?" April started. "I mean, at your age, have you ever had heart problems?"

Jones smiled and slowly slid to a sitting position. "Don't worry. I'm not having a heart attack. It was just such a shock."

"I'm truly sorry to burden you with this," April said.

"No," the man said, a new strength in his voice. "I thank God that you came to me." His face turned stern. "You see, my grandson just turned ten." Anger replaced his former shock. "He's one of Brother Ralph's favorites."

April looked at the man before her and prayed with all her heart that Adora had been lying. Even as she prayed she knew the transsexual's words had been true. It would be a long road for Alfred Jones's grandson, a long road to recovery.

⁂

April felt odd as she slipped the key into the lock. She wasn't yet comfortable letting herself into Sophia's house. Slider stood close behind her, a soft-sided carry-on case over his shoulder and a suitcase in one hand.

"Hurry up. This shit's heavy," he said.

"Patience, I haven't gotten the hang of this lock," April answered as she fiddled with the door, balancing the laptop bag resting between her feet.

The door opened abruptly, and Sophia stood in the doorway, a light of relief in her eyes.

"*Bien venidos*, I cannot tell you how glad I am to have you safely home."

"So it's home now?" Slider whispered.

April swung her fist over her shoulder, punching her friend in the middle of his chest and causing Slider to end his question with a surprised and breathless hrumph.

"I'm glad to see you, too," April said to the dark-eyed woman.

"Hey, these bags are still heavy," Slider commented

Sophia stood aside so April and Slider could enter.

"Just take the bags upstairs to my room," Sophia instructed.

Slider smirked and then moved rapidly up the steps to avoid any possibility of April's next punch. He barely felt the scathing look that followed him. April's distress with her best friend and his teasing evaporated at the feel of Sophia's gentle fingers massaging her neck.

"How are you holding up with all this?" Sophia asked.

April turned to take the Latina in her arms, and they kissed…long, slow, and with a great deal of pleasure.

"I'm much better now, April answered.

Slider cleared his throat loudly and began whistling a poor attempt at the "Star-Spangled Banner" as he started down the stairs. He paused at the bottom and stared at the pair with an ear-to-ear grin.

"Am I interrupting anything?" Slider asked.

April sighed. "Slider I may interrupt your butt with my boot if you don't knock it off."

Slider dropped to a seat in an armchair. "Hey, teasing is just an expression of love and concern."

April stepped behind him, wrapped her arm around his throat and rubbed her knuckles across the thinning hair of his scalp. "So are nuggies," she responded. At that moment Nearly jumped in Slider's lap and nosed and licked his way around Slider's face and April's hands.

"Hey! I'm drowning here!" Slider called as he flayed long arms in a halfhearted attempt at protecting himself.

April backed away, laughing. "Off him, Nearly. As much fun as it may be, even Slider can take only so much abuse." The dog happily deserted Slider to stand with his two front paws on his mistress's stomach while she searched for all the itchy spots. Nearly's tail thumped against the chair, a sure sign of happiness. Sophia now watched from a comfortable seat on the couch, and as April looked at the smiling woman, April felt the tail wagging in her own heart.

"Slider, it's time for you to go home," April said.

"What?" Slider sputtered in mock frustration. "I just got here."

"I'll buy you lunch tomorrow, buddy, but now it's time to go home."

A sly grin covered Slider's face. "What could you two possible do without me that you couldn't do with me?"

"I love you, Slider. Now out!"

Slider uncoiled from his slouch in the chair and started for the door. "Okay, but this definitely means lunch."

"Deal," April responded as she closed the door behind him.

April rested in Sophia's arms even before Slider started his car. As they kissed, April felt her pulse quicken. She pushed away, gently.

"Wait a minute while we still can," April said.

Sophia raised April's hand to her lips and nibbled at the fingers. "Why?"

"Because there have been some major developments, and I haven't had a chance to update you."

Abruptly, the attorney returned and the seductress...well the seductress could wait. "What's happened?" Sophia asked, her voice all business.

"Met an interesting person named Adora earlier

today."

"Tell me more."

April shared the whole tale, Sophia listening with fascination.

"*Madre de Dios*," she responded as April told of Alfred Jones' grandson. "What's Mr. Jones going to do?" she asked.

"Go to talk with Sergeant Folkers. They'll probably question the grandson, and I'm sure the police will want a physical examination."

"How horrible for the boy."

"Not as horrible as years of continued abuse. Besides, there's an organization in town that specializes in making the whole process as easy as possible for a child. I know the folks, they're gentle and caring. They'll do the best they can for him."

For the first time since entering the house, April noticed the stack of reading material on the coffee table. There were PFLAG brochures, books including *Is It a Choice*, and *Lesbian Path*.

"What's this?" April asked.

Sophia moved close to April, nestling her head on the other woman's shoulder. "I'm in love with a woman. I'd better learn what it means to be a lesbian."

April's laugh ended as Sophia place her lips over April's mouth, the beginning of a wonderful end to a difficult day.

Chapter Thirteen

April awoke to the scent of vanilla and the smooth touch of soft skin against her cheek. Pleasure greeted her as she slowly drifted from sleep to consciousness. Even in their sleep, April and Sophia maintained touch, and April awoke to morning light with her body curled perfectly around the sleeping form of her lover. April couldn't remember the last time she had known such peace, such gentle pleasure.

She nuzzled at the back of her lover's neck, enjoying the tickle of soft, dark hair against her face. Sophia moaned pleasurably and rolled toward April, while April continued to nuzzle her way from the back of Sophia's neck to the base of her jaw. April nibbled at her lover's chin and mouth, enjoying the smell of her intimate scent, still present from their lovemaking the night before. April's amazement at the ease with which Sophia adapted to sex with a woman only added to her pleasure.

Sophia smiled sleepily, not yet opening her eyes. "I thought we were sleeping in," the Latina said.

April raised on one elbow and looked at the clock on Sophia's nightstand. The numbers read eight thirty in an intrusive, glaring orange.

"We have," April responded.

Sophia reluctantly opened her eyes, eyebrows raised skeptically, as she moved her head so that she, too, could see the clock.

"If this is sleeping in to a journalist, this attorney may need to make a case for earlier nights."

April laughed deep in her throat as she returned to nuzzling her lover's neck. She barely stopped her light kisses to speak against the soft skin. "We were in bed plenty early."

Sophia laughed. "Excuse me. Let me clarify. I'm referring to sleep."

Sophia rolled onto her side, facing April, and they both shifted easily until their bodies fit comfortably together, the sensation of skin against skin optimized. They easily found the rhythm of their kisses. April learned from experience that sometimes two people's tongues and mouths danced to the same music and sometimes they did not. Sophia and April easily matched pace and intensity like a well-practiced couple on the dance floor. Their kisses began slow, rhythmic, and smooth and, even the first time, they'd intuitively sensed as each partner readied to progress in intensity and passion. There was no hurry. For now, they simply enjoyed each other.

"We could be sleeping," Sophia whispered.

"Yes, we could." April continued the kiss between words.

In a fluid motion, Sophia pulled April atop her, and, for a moment, they both lay still, simply feeling the other's heartbeat against their own chest. April felt an intensity of intimacy she had rarely, if ever, known before. They both enjoyed one of those rare moments when they truly knew they did not live alone in the universe.

Riiiiiiiing!

Without any apparent effort, April jumped straight up and landed in a sitting position beside where Sophia lay wide-eyed.

"Damn." April said.

Riiiiing!

"Do you usually get calls this early on Sunday?"

"No," Sophia responded as she rolled over to answer the cordless phone on the bedside table. April placed her hand on her bare chest, trying to still her heart, now beating rapidly with surprise rather than passion. Sophia turned, holding the receiver toward April.

"It's for you," Sophia said.

"Me?" April took the phone.

"Hey, Sims. It's Frank Folkers," the voice said on the other end of the line. "I've been trying to call your cell phone."

"Yeah, I…I wanted to sleep so I turned it off."

"Sure. I hear you. Been kind of tough lately. You need some rest," Folkers responded.

"Sergeant. I figured it was Slider. I nearly forgot I gave you this number."

The policeman's voice sounded fuzzy with fatigue. "Yeah, well I didn't forget the number. That's what matters." April could hear the slurp of coffee. "Sorry to bother you so early, but I'd like for you to come down to the station."

"What's up?"

"I'll tell you when you get here. I will say one thing, you sure know how to open a kettle of worms, lady."

"And I leave you to work all night sorting the fishing worms from the throwbacks, right?"

"Right," the sergeant responded. "Now that you've had your beauty rest, I'd like you here. Was that your attorney…friend who answered the phone?"

"Yes."

"Bring her, too. I've got some folks here who'd like to talk with an attorney they can trust."

"Do they know her?" April asked.

"No, but they sure seem to think you've hung the moon. If you tell them she's okay, they'll trust her."

"Who's there?" April asked, curious.

"Just get your butt down to the station," the sergeant said, losing patience. "Every minute I waste talking with you means one more minute before I can go home to bed."

"Sorry, Frank. We'll be there as soon as we can."

April explained what little she knew as she dressed in the clothes she'd worn the night before, pausing to throw Sophia's clothes, also from the day before, toward her lover. Despite a pause for both of them to thoroughly wash faces and hands (some scents should not be carried into a police station), they were dressed and downtown within a half hour of Sergeant Folker's call. The detective looked just as bad as he'd sounded on the phone, as April and Sophia walked toward him. Seated in the chairs in front of Folker's desk, were a haggard Alfred Jones beside a younger version of himself. They both looked tired, but were dressed in fresh clothes and clean-shaven. They may have lost sleep, but they hadn't spent the night at the station.

Mr. Jones stood, offering his hand to April. "I'm very glad to see you." The tears teasing at his eyes surprised both women. "April Sims, I want you to meet my son, Roger."

April shook the younger man's hand then introduced Sophia as her friend and an attorney.

"You're the attorney the sergeant mentioned,"

the younger man said.

"Yes," Sophia answered.

Roger's fists clenched and unclenched, his face grew white with anger. "We'll file every charge we can, but we want to talk to you about a civil case," he said.

April and Sophia glanced at each other, confirming their mutual confusion.

"File charges against whom, about what?" Sophia asked.

A painful silence followed.

Confusion disappeared as April looked at the two men, abruptly understanding their distress and anger.

"Thomas. It's Thomas, isn't it?"

The older man's hands shook, and the younger man put a hand under his father' elbow.

"Dad, take it easy."

April's face flushed with furry. "Your grandson?"

"The Jones boy and at least three others that we now know about," Folkers interrupted.

"That sorry son of bitch," April said. She glanced at the two men. "Sorry. I didn't mean to offend you."

"No offense," Alfred responded. "This is a rare time when I wish I'd learned to swear."

Sophia leaned forward, placing her hand on Roger's arm. "I'll do everything I can to help. The stronger the action, the better the likelihood that he can be prevented from ever doing it again."

"Where's your grandson?" April asked.

"At home with his mother, grandmother, and sister."

Folkers drank the last of his cold coffee. "We took all the boys to The Bridge yesterday," he said.

"The Bridge?" Sophia asked.

"It's a place that specializes in questioning and examining children believed to have been…" April glanced at Alfred and Roger, regretting any pain her bluntness may cause.

"Sexually abused," Roger completed her sentence, the cold fury apparent in the flatness of his voice.

"The folks at The Bridge are great," Sergeant Folkers said. "They make it as easy as possible on the kids while getting the best information possible to make a case."

"Can you make a case?" Sophia asked.

The sergeant leaned forward, ice reflected in his red-rimmed eyes. "We got the bastard cold." The policeman glanced at the two men. "Sorry, you know us policemen and reporters and our language."

Roger looked directly at April. "I don't think I've got a right to judge anybody when I didn't even protect my own son from a snake like Brother Thomas." The man buried his face in his hands and sobbed.

Alfred placed his arm around the young man. "Son, don't blame yourself. We all thought Brother Thomas…"

"Not you, Dad." the son responded. "You questioned him. You knew better, but I was a fool. He was so…dynamic and it felt so good to be one of his warriors for Christ." The young man looked at April and Sophia and then studied the ends of his shoes. "I'm so very sorry. I…I was one of the men at your friend's bar the night we…the night we…"

"Trashed the place," April responded.

"Yes," Roger answered.

"Son," Alfred said, hurt and surprised.

"I know, Dad. I should have listened to you."

April looked to Sophia as they both thought how to respond.

"I guess we've all been fools sometime," April said. "The important thing is that you learn better."

"Paying damages might be a good start to proving you've learned a lesson," Sophia said, ever the practical attorney.

The young man looked at the two women with torment in his eyes. "I don't care if I have to sell everything I own, I'll pay every nickel of damage, medical costs, too."

Sergeant Folkers looked at April. "Do you think Tandy will want to press charges?"

April studied the tormented young man before her. "We'll need to talk to her, but I don't think she'll see Roger as a man who needs a police record haunting him and his family."

"What about the other men?" Folkers asked.

"Other men? You want me to tell you who the others were?" Roger asked.

"Whoa, Frank. Let's take this one step at a time," April responded.

The sergeant rubbed tired eyes. "Sounds good to me."

"Where's Thomas?" Sophia asked.

The detective's eyes narrowed and his lips curved in a frightening hint of a smile. "Holding cell. Been there all night."

April's face reflected his smile. "Open cell block?"

"Yep."

"I don't understand," Alfred said.

"Child mol...people who abuse children aren't very popular, even among the city's criminal community," April answered.

Roger giggled. April realized he was near to losing control. "You mean, he spent the night dealing with people who hate what he did?"

"Who hate what he did, and who don't mind letting him know about it," the sergeant answered.

"What Brother Thomas did is not right, but neither is vindictiveness," Alfred Jones interrupted.

April looked at the man, wondering if she'd ever known anyone who lived their convictions as completely as this man. "You're right, Alfred. You're very right," she said.

"Can we have Brother Thomas removed from this...?"

"Holding cell," Sergeant Folkers said.

"Yes."

"Already done. After a few hours in the holding cell, your Brother Thomas asked for me, and I took his full confession at 3 a.m. He's now comfortably in a semiprivate cell where he'll most likely be until trial and transfer to Huntsville."

April looked at the two tired and tormented men. "Do you need us any more, Frank?"

"I need you to get out of here so I can go home and sleep."

"Done," April responded. She looked at the Joneses. "Forgive me for butting in, but neither of you really looks fit to drive. Why don't I drive you home, and Sophia can follow me to your house? I'm sure your grandson would like to have you there."

"That would be good," Alfred responded. "When you first told me what you suspected, I'm...I'm sorry I..."

"Don't. I'd have been worried if you hadn't

questioned me," April said.

Sophia stood, her car keys now in hand. "Gentlemen. Go home. Your families need you."

They rode in silence down the elevator and the atmosphere remained quiet and somber as they walked to their cars. Alfred was so tired that he was snoring in the backseat before they left the parking lot. Roger used single words and short phrases to direct April to his home, while Sophia followed closely behind.

"Are you…are you a…" Roger tried to ask.

"Am I a lesbian?" April responded.

"Yes."

"I'm a for real, card-carrying dyke."

"The woman back there, the attorney…is she your…"

"My lover. Yes."

Roger looked at his hands for a long time, almost forgetting to tell April which exit she needed.

"You know, Brother Thomas said all homosexuals are servants of Satan," Roger said.

"Now that you're sitting beside a for real homosexual, what do you think?" April asked.

Roger looked at her long and hard. "I think Dad's right."

"What does he say?

"That we're all God's children, and it's up to Him to decide who's right and who's wrong."

"I like your dad." April gave Roger a sideways glance. "Okay, so you'll listen to your dad, but I want to know what you think."

The man raised his head and looked at her. "I think you stuck your neck out to help protect my son." He reached across to place a hand on April's shoulder. "I think I like and respect a homosexual."

"Hallelujah," April said.

Except for an occasional direction from her passenger, the rest of the drive was spent in silence. It was a comfortable silence.

Chapter Fourteen

W hat's this?" Johnnie asked, her lip curled in a sneer.

April glanced at the plate in her hand. "What's it look like? It's cheese and crackers."

"Last time I saw you bring plain cheese and crackers was over a year ago before..." Johnnie closed one eye and squinted the other as she struggled to remember. "Ah, that's it. Sophia work late tonight?"

"Yeah, so what?" April demanded.

Johnnie sighed as she glanced at the plate covered in saltines and uneven slices of Monterey Jack. "Oh well, there's always next week for Sophia's *chili con queso*."

April, only slightly huffy, plopped her plate on the table and motioned at the other dishes already there. "What you think? We're going to starve to death."

Billboard laughed until crumbs escaped from a mouth filled with tidbits while she filled her plate with larger chunks. "Fat chance," she said between chews. She paused to swallow the mouthful. "I swear, the spread gets better every time."

"You still mad there's no beer?" April asked.

"What?" Billboard responded.

"Yeah, you remember," Johnnie added. "At that first meeting."

Billboard laughed. "I'd forgotten." She cocked

her head to one side thinking. "Guys, I used to drink a lot more beer than I do now, didn't I?"

"That's putting it mildly," Mo added, slapping Billboard on the shoulder. "There was a time when you guaranteed death to any six-pack."

"Six-pack, my ass," Johnnie said. "She'd mortally wound a case."

Billboard blushed as she carried her plate from the table, making room for others waiting to fill theirs. "Knock it off, guys."

Johnnie grabbed the larger woman around the waist and hugged her tightly. "Billboard, we wouldn't tease you if we didn't love you."

Her friends watched in surprise as Billboard Sally blinked back tears. "Yeah, I know."

In the mill of people, the old group drifted to separate corners, welcoming the newcomers. April paused to look around the room. The same old couches nearly groaned under the weight of newcomers, but new upholstery, sewn by Johnnie's own hands, gave them the look of new. Ratty old tables and chairs had been painted or replaced. New curtains, provided by the men's group that now met on Thursday nights, adorned the windows and a fresh coat of paint covered the once dingy walls. She studied the room, trying to remember the dusty hull she'd seen the first time Tandy escorted her up the steps. In not much over a year, the Ladies' Room took on a life of its own. Tandy's dream had come true. Thirty to forty women filled the place each Tuesday night, and they had begun the search for a new site to accommodate the growing group. April had long since given up the role of facilitator. Now, a committee performed the task, arranging a variety of programs, topics and activities. Occasionally, they received official requests from public agencies, asking for an opportunity to speak to the group. The health department recruited women for health screening, focusing on mammograms and educating the group on the higher statistical risk of breast cancer among lesbians. Contacts made during that session, and during the session on sexually transmitted diseases for both the Ladies' and the Men's Rooms, resulted in expansion of the local AIDS support organization. The Lambda AA had formed just four months earlier and now used the room each Wednesday evening and Saturday morning.

"Sooooo, where is that gorgeous partner of yours?" Johnnie asked.

"She'll be here. I came early to open up, and she went to pick up our program for the night."

"Who is it?"

April smiled. "It's a surprise."

Johnnie moaned. "Come on April. I'm not up to another session on breast cancer. Do you realize how many leftovers we had that night?"

"That one nurse looked like she was going to die of embarrassment when Sandy and Billboard started having fun feeling all the artificial breasts."

Johnnie laughed. "I thought I'd bust a gut when Sandy said the demos were very realistic if they could just make them a little warmer."

"I thought Stella was going to kill her," April recalled.

"Give, my friend. What's tonight's program?" Johnnie demanded.

The door opened, rescuing April from an answer. April still felt her heart rate increase as she watched her lover enter the room. April walked to Sophia, and they kissed, briefly, just a hint of the real warmth of welcome they both felt. The kiss was especially restrained out of respect for the older couple entering the room behind Sophia.

"How you doing, Alfred?" April asked. She gave the man a warm hug, one he gratefully returned. "And you, Martha?" she added as she turned to Alfred's wife. In the past year, April and Sophia had grown to love this woman, the companion to the man who had the courage to face Ralph Thomas. The wrinkles around her eyes and the gray nearly hiding the auburn of her hair barely hid the beauty she had been as a young woman. Sophia once said she saw more beauty in the character of the older woman's face than any younger woman could ever display. April agreed. In many ways, Martha Jones had become a mother to them both.

The room had gone quiet at the arrival of the couple, and April turned to face the expectant group. "Everyone, I want you to meet Alfred and Martha Jones. Some of you may remember them."

"I know them," Terry called. Her voice was a far cry from the frightened young woman she'd once been. Strong and confident, she faced the members of her former church without fear.

Martha gasped with pleasure and moved to a seat beside young Terry. The older woman hugged the younger.

"Dear Terry. It's so good to see you. I cannot tell you how much you've been on my heart."

Terry blinked back tears. "I...I'm glad to have a chance to thank you and Mr. Jones for all you did to stop...to stop..."

"It's all right, dear. I just regret letting him hurt

you so badly."

Terry placed her hand over Martha's. "I…I grew up a lot. Something good came of it all. I don't regret where I am now."

April cleared her throat and motioned for Alfred to take a seat near his wife. The man set a briefcase at his feet.

"Alfred and Martha asked to speak to the Ladies' Room tonight. They're starting a new organization, and they want our help."

Alfred opened the briefcase and circulated handfuls of brochures. "I'm certain most of you are familiar with PFLAG, but my wife and I only learned of the organization a few weeks ago. I'm sending around the room one of the brochures provided by the national PFLAG organization."

The room fell silent as the women studied the brochures. "This looks great, but why did you want to talk with us?" Sandy asked.

Alfred and Martha shared a glance, a glance that communicated a level of commitment they shared. "Mr. Jones and I have decided to start a chapter of PFLAG here in Amber. First, know that any of you who wish to attend PFLAG meetings are welcome, but we also want you to spread the word to your families and friends."

"Hot ziggidy dog," Mo called. She looked at her sister. "Alli, now you don't have to hang out with lesbians all the time just to show you love your sister."

Allison slapped her sister on the knee and smiled at the older couple. "My sister may be a little crass, but she is correct. I'm thrilled you're starting a PFLAG, and you can know that I'll do all I can to help."

One of the newcomers looked toward Alfred.

"I'm really pleased someone's going to do this, but what made you two decide to be the ones?"

Alfred looked at April. "Not more than a year ago, I was among those who persecuted you, a staunch member of a conservative church."

"What made you change your mind?"

Alfred smiled, a touch of sadness to that smile. "Perhaps it would help if I told our story," he said.

April leaned back, taking her lover's hand in her own, waiting to hear a tale she already knew. Sophia's fingers snuggled warmly, and April felt a peace she did not think she'd ever known before. She listened to a man she respected while sitting beside the woman she loved. All in all, it had been a very good year.

About the Author

Kayt C. Peck claims the work she did helping form OUTstanding Amarillo in the 1990s as one of the proudest periods of her life. With a handful of courageous leaders, they openly faced prejudice and persecution that, at that time, was largely sanctioned by the local status quo. They helped change that attitude. Despite her years as an officer in the Naval Reserve, she believes OUTstanding was her most important life effort in fighting for the basic principle of Freedom. That experience helped inspire creation of The Ladies' Room. During her writing career, Peck has published three other novels, one biography, and written a number of plays including "Sheltered Women," the 2015 winner of the New Mexico AACTFest. She has authored and published numerous articles, short-stories and poems. Today, she lives quietly in her cabin home in the mountains of northeastern New Mexico.

Other title available by Kayt C. Peck

Good Water- ISBN- 978-1-939062-87-1

The dry plains drew Judy Proctor like a bear to her den…or a moth to the flame. Ranching was her life. The sweat as she branded or "doctored" cattle…the howl of a coyote in the quiet, night air… half-frozen fingers as she cut the wire to loosen hay bales for hungry cattle scratching for survival in snow-covered land…all of the everyday existence on the ranch was her life.
It was where she belonged.
It was a lonely life.

She had tried to leave the ranch to join the "normal" existence of a talented young woman in the city, but it had never been home. When her parents were killed in an automobile accident, she returned to the family ranch as much because she needed it as it needed her. She faced a lonely life to be shared with no better company than Somegood and Useless, her cow dog and the mottled mutt that were her companions.

Kathleen Romero slipped into Judy's life unexpectedly. She came to the plains to write a story. Would she stay because of the real truth she found in the simple drama of husbanding land and animals?

Unfortunately, even wide-open spaces can be plagued by prejudice and closed-minds. As the two women struggle to know each other, they must also carve a place for themselves among the country-folk who have been Judy's friends and neighbors her entire life.

Other titles available by Sapphire Books Publishing

Deception by Design – ISBN – 978-1-939062-91-8

Photographer Joshlyn Davis moves through her life drawing as little attention as possible. She longs for the simple life with few complications and the less people know her the better. The long buried secrets have taken a toll, but everything is just how she wants it, or so she thought. Graphic/Software designer Kellen Reynolds lives her days substantiating her work from home business and her nights burning up the pavement at the local amateur race track. There really hadn't been much thought of a private life until a chance meeting with Joshlyn Davis. Almost immediately Kellen and Joshlyn find a connection and begin to slowly explore a relationship. Will the relationship have time to develop or will something dark and sinister put an end to it?

Beyond the Garden – ISBN - 978-1-943353-01-9

Life as an immortal is never easy. For Lilith, it's become almost intolerable. Her only goal now, to find a way to die. Her quest takes her across the globe and back again. When she meets master scuba diver Dana Reed, her goal is turned upside down. Dana offers her a breathtaking romance, as long as destiny cooperates.

Hell hounds, archeological booby traps and self-appointed fanatics serve as a backdrop for this romantic adventure. The results could be disastrous or more wondrous than she ever imagined. It's up to Lilith to decide her path and fight through to realize her dreams.

Future Promises – ISBN – 978-1-943353-03-3

Rose Thomas has spent the last few years riding horses and mending fences at a women's only dude ranch. Life is going great for the wrangler until she receives news of the passing of a relative. The journey home leaves her with new options for her future and a handful of journals that were written during the Civil War. Now she gets to read about the stories that she had listened to growing up, but as she turns the pages, she realizes some things had changed over time.

Keri Masters has spent her life trying to make her parents and her boyfriend of eight years happy. Before she is set to join her parents and their medical practice, she has a few things she needs to do: break up with her boyfriend and take a long overdue trip west. When she arrives at the dude ranch, she is drawn to Rose and is forced to face feelings she hasn't acknowledge for a long time.

Under the hot Arizona sun, Rose and Keri's feelings for each other start to heat up, as does the story in the pages that Rose continues to read. But as the two women grow closer, their time together is cut short. Will Rose find a happy ending between the pages of the journal, and will she and Keri be able to find their own happy ending?

To Love Again – ISBN – 978-1-939062-99-4

Jade Donovan felt like she had everything in life, a great marriage, a beautiful daughter, and then fate intervened. Now she needs to learn how to move forward, not only for herself, but her four-year-old daughter. Jade's best friend Kristel hopes to help her get back on track by attending a grief counseling group run by Rachel Cassidy, a widow herself. With time, Jade is able to take the steps forward to heal and finds herself falling for Rachel. Not everybody is happy with the path that Jade has started on. Will Jade be able to overcome the loss of her wife and the other obstacles life has in store for her, to be able To Love Again?

Undone – ISBN – 978-1-939062-77-2

Poetry by its very nature should be fully experiential, create imagery, becoming visceral and evocative of emotion. The very nature of the poem exists in the sensual world and, thus, it is erotic at the core. In poetry, I hear the words lyrically, as spoken, perhaps even whispered or sung; I see images as they create patterns of meaning in meter - and I see the face of my lover. Hopefully, you will experience these poems as instances of sensuous experience in words spoken aloud with a lover.

9 781943 353095